SARAH AND THE MYSTERY OF THE
HIDDEN BOY

Winner Books are produced by Victor Books and are
designed to entertain and instruct young readers in
Christian principles. Each book has been approved by
specialists in Christian education and children's litera-
ture. These books uphold the teachings and principles
of the Bible.

Other Winner Books you will enjoy:
Sarah and the Magic Twenty-fifth, by Margaret Epp
Sarah and the Pelican, by Margaret Epp
Sarah and the Lost Friendship, by Margaret Epp
The Hairy Brown Angel and Other Animal Tails, ed-
    ited by Grace Fox Anderson
Danger on the Alaskan Trail (three stories)
Gopher Hole Treasure Hunt, by Ralph Bartholomew
Daddy, Come Home, by Irene Aiken
Patches, by Edith V. Buck
Battle at the Blue Line, by P. C. Fredricks
The Peanut Butter Hamster and Other Animals Tails,
    edited by Grace Fox Anderson
The Taming of Cheetah, by Lee Roddy

MARGARET EPP was born into a large family in Waldheim, Saskatchewan. She spent six years of her early childhood in China, where her parents served as missionaries with the China Mennonite Mission Society. Illness forced them to return to Canada, where they settled on a farm.

Miss Epp is a graduate of Bethany Bible Institute in Hepburn, Saskatchewan, and attended Prairie Bible Institute, Three Hills, Alberta. For 30 years she has specialized in writing books for children and young people.

SARAH AND THE MYSTERY OF THE HIDDEN BOY

MARGARET EPP

A WINNER BOOK

VICTOR BOOKS

a division of SP Publications, Inc., Wheaton, Illinois
Offices also in Fullerton, California • Whitby, Ontario, Canada • London, England

All Scripture quotations are from the King James Version.

Library of Congress Catalog Card No. 79-65043
ISBN: 0-88207-485-7

VICTOR BOOKS
A division of SP Publications, Inc.
P.O. Box 1825, Wheaton, Ill. 60187

CONTENTS

1 Friends—Old and New   7
2 Bouncer Makes a Choice   21
3 An Arrival and a Mystery   32
4 Unexpected Happenings   45
5 Sarah Turns Detective   55
6 New Boy at Braeburn   69
7 A Surprise for Sarah   82
8 Sarah Takes Charge   96
9 Back to School   105
10 Ivan to the Rescue   123
11 What Sarah Learned   135

CHAPTER 1

FRIENDS—OLD AND NEW

SPRING MUD is deep, and mucky, and treacherous. That's why Sarah Scott let her brother Robbie ride ahead of her on the way home from school. His horse, Wally, wasn't nearly as nice as her own Blackie. When roads were dry and smooth Blackie carried her along, smooth as a swallow's flight.

Wally was—Wally. A lumbering, clumsy-looking horse. *But* he had horse sense. He knew how to pick places where there was good solid footing. That was what he was doing today.

In spite of the mud, Sarah's heart sang this Friday evening in April 1926. For two weeks, ever since her eleventh birthday, Blackie had belonged to her. The horse was a birthday present from three important people—from Linda Bolton, Sarah's very best friend. From Linda's dad, who was a diplomat in Ottawa, and from his sister, Aunt Jane Bolton.

Actually, Aunt Jane wasn't any relation at all to the Scott family. But both Sarah and Robbie had called her Aunt Jane for many years.

Last summer, on a special but rather dreadful day, Aunt

Jane plunged down a flight of stairs in her house, and lay unconscious with a broken hip. The only other person there was Linda—but she was crippled then from polio. She couldn't do a thing. She couldn't even use the telephone to call for help.

Then Sarah came.

Blackie was a reminder of that day. She was a big, live thank-you from all of the Boltons.

"But I didn't do anything special, nothing heroic," thought Sarah for the 50th time as she and Robbie trotted past Aunt Jane's neat driveway.

The road ran over a slight hill here. It was almost dry. Wally and Blackie broke into a canter. Sarah felt the spring wind on her cheeks. She shook back her hair and laughed. "Beat you home," she challenged. "Hi up there, Blackie!"

"Hey, you, Wally! Shake a leg!" yelled Robbie. "We can't let the girls beat us."

And now they were racing each other. Over the dry stretches, through shallow puddles, slithering in muddy patches, with big blobs flying through the air. Then they were pounding along the grass strip that ran beside the trail.

They were nearing home. The horses enjoyed this as much as their riders. Only one person was missing in the fun. That was Spencer, their handsome collie.

As far back as Sarah remembered, he had come hurtling to meet them when they returned from school. Summer and winter, springtime and fall, he was always there to welcome them. He must be getting lazy. This was the fourth time in a row that he hadn't at least trotted to the roadway to greet them.

For the next half hour Sarah forgot about Spencer. She and Robbie had to clean their horses and brush them down in the barn. This was one job no one would do for Sarah. It went with owning a horse, said father. An owner is responsible for the comfort, health, and appearance of his animal.

Sarah was getting pretty good at the job. Still, Robbie finished a few minutes ahead of her. He went to the harness room to put away the brush and cloths and pail. The first inkling Sarah had that something was wrong was when Robbie came back suddenly, half stumbling. As if his legs couldn't carry him! There was a slack look on his face. "Come, look," he said in a queer voice.

A shaft of sunlight had moved along the floor of the barn. It rested now on a curled-up mop of white and yellow and bronze hair—Spencer.

"Not—*dead!*" whispered Sarah with a catch in her throat.

But he was. The collie's head lay on an old coat of Robbie's, and that seemed especially fitting. He came to the Scott farm when Robbie was a baby—almost three years before Sarah was born. All their lives the boy and dog had been special friends. For a dog, Spencer was old, old. But only the last few weeks had he seemed to age.

Sarah, her heart bursting in her throat, raced to the house to tell the rest of the family—Father, Mother, and big brother Keith. Her other brother Stuart, who drove to high school in town every day, came home just when the family was crowding into the little harness room, to see the empty mop that used to be a loving, lively, loyal friend.

Father and Keith took spades and went to find a good spot for a grave in the orchard. But it was Robbie who took the bundle of fur in his arms and carried it all the way.

At suppertime everyone tried to be cheerful. But Sarah had a lost feeling inside. She remembered—oh, so many things. How he used to frisk and frolic with them. He would plunge alongside when they went coasting down the hill in winter. He went swimming in the creek with them in summer.

When she was home alone during a furious blizzard last fall, he kept her company. Ordinarily you couldn't drag him indoors, unless there was a thunderstorm. But that day he had whined to come in. Later, he whined again to go into the storm. His barking outdoors came just in time to save Robbie's life! Without it, Robbie said, he would have been lost in the howling storm.

She remembered the time she was sick last winter. For days she was delirious. And all that time, Spencer lay as close to the door as possible. He wouldn't budge until she was well enough to go to the door and speak to him. Then he went wild, just plain silly wild, with joy.

She remembered what Father said not so long ago—and she thought now that he must have meant to warn them. He was talking about Robbie—and Spencer.

"Fourteen is the beginning for a boy. But it's nearing the end for a dog."

Well, today was the end. It was like reading a lovely, thick book, thought Sarah. You want it to go on and never end. But finally you turn the last page.

"Has anyone heard of a likely pup?" Father asked.

"Grant Millar—" began Keith.

"Who wants a pesky pup around the place?" Robbie broke in, his voice husky.

"A farm needs a dog," Father answered mildly. "We should have had one in training long ago."

Just then they heard the slow rattle of a wagon coming into the yard. Tonight there was no Spencer to bark a warning or a welcome. A man and a woman sat high on the seat of the wagon.

"The Chernishenkos," said Father.

That was the name of Aunt Jane Bolton's new hired man. All the Scotts turned out to welcome their new neighbors.

The Ukrainian couple had gone to the nearest big town—Paxton—to buy secondhand furniture for their home. This morning they borrowed the Scott wagon for that purpose. Father and Sarah's three brothers stood on Mr. Chernishenko's side of the wagon. Mother, with her apron wrapped around her arms for warmth, stood talking with the plump lady. Mother had to speak slowly, in short simple sentences. Mrs. Chernishenko had come to Canada only a few months before. She spoke only a little English.

She must love colors—all mixed together. Her sweater was dark red, more like maroon, really. Her blouse was pink. Her skirt, all frilly, was orange. A black scarf covered her head, but it was embroidered in blue and red and yellow. All over! And most interesting of all, her white stockings were covered with embroidered flowers.

The load behind the couple looked as higgeldy-piggeldy as Mrs. Chernishenko's clothes, thought Sarah. By craning her neck, she could see a wash boiler, a cupboard, a washstand, a couple of overturned chairs with their legs sticking up, and a mattress riding on the legs. She hopped onto the axle of the large wheel, and from there to the side step for a better look.

"Nuh!" Mrs. Chernishenko had swung around. She gave Sarah a little push. "Nuh! Not goot!"

"Sarah!" exclaimed Mother, embarrassed.

Sarah dropped to the ground. Her face felt fiery red.

"Goot girl, goot girl," said Mrs. Chernishenko, now smiling and trying to be friendly.

But Sarah raced toward the house to get out of sight. In the kitchen she scraped the supper plates and stacked them. And *still* Mother and Father stood talking with their new neighbors. Sarah filled the dishpan with hot water from the boxlike tank on the side of the cookstove. She had almost finished rinsing the washed dishes when her parents came back indoors.

"Hey! Who's working so hard?" exclaimed Father. And he reached for the dishtowel. "And why so silent, Princess?"

"I wasn't doing anything!" Sarah burst out. "Just looking at the junky old stuff. Why did she have to get fussed about that?"

Father seldom laughed aloud, but his shoulders were shaking. "She's her mother's daughter, Sheila. It's the Irish in you. The madder you get, the harder you work."

"You just hush up, John," said Mother. But there was a twinkle in her eyes. "Sarah, you have no call to be angry with Mrs. Chernishenko. You *were* poking into matters that did not exactly concern you. Besides, she sent you a present as peace-offering."

Two apple tarts were wrapped in a piece of newspaper. And in a nest of colored straw sat a beautifully colored Easter egg. Oh, fancy as could be! Sarah forgave Mrs. Chernishenko —and she ate one of the tarts—all juicy and crumbly and good. She saved the other for Robbie. He was so silent and sad tonight.

That night, Spencer's little home was empty. Ginger, the cat, Spencer's special pal, always slept between his paws. She mewed half the night with lonesomeness. Sarah shed no tears, but she was crying inside.

Monday was a big day. Arbor Day at school, pig butchering day at home. Blackie stayed home because Sarah and Robbie could not ride horseback and carry all the things they would need at school. They had to take the buggy to hold the rakes and pails, a scrubbing brush, old cloths, and their lunch pails. So they rattled away in the buggy with Wally between the shafts in front and rake handles sticking out behind.

Almost before they reached the road, two cars breezed past

into the yard. The Gerricks first. Ever since Sarah's big sister, Kathleen, married Herbie Gerrick last fall, and went off to California with him, the two families sort of stuck together. They always helped each other at special family occasions, like birthdays, wood sawing, threshing, and pig-butchering— things like that.

The second car was driven by Aunt Jane Bolton. Her new hired man and his wife, the Chernishenkos, sat in the back. Mrs. Chernishenko was clutching the seatback in front of her. She looked worried and excited. It reminded Sarah of yesterday—Sunday.

For the first time in many years Aunt Jane had gone to Braeburn church.

You could hardly tell that her hip had been broken, though she carried a cane to keep her from stumbling. Her back was as straight as ever. Aunt Jane said that a broken hip was a small price to pay for a mended heart. Because of her illness, she had come back to God!

With flushed cheeks, she had walked bravely up the steps and into the church, looking straight ahead. Brother and Sister Hammond, the minister and his wife, came smiling to welcome her and the Chernishenkos. That must have helped some. But not everyone was friendly.

In a way Sarah could understand why people didn't crowd around to shake hands with the Ukrainian couple. The lady wore the same outfit she wore the other night, except that her sweater was bright green instead of maroon. In her old home, in the Ukraine, she would look very fine and fancy. Here she looked—odd. But people weren't noticing her nearly as much as they noticed Aunt Jane.

Sarah heard one big girl mutter, "Imagine! Old Miss High and Mighty coming to church with hired help! What next?"

And someone else said, with a laugh, "I bet she's brought

those Rooshians so people won't stare so much at her." Sarah was almost sure Aunt Jane had heard because her cheeks turned a deeper red.

Sarah felt proud of her best Braeburn friend, Susan Gerrick. Susan nudged Sarah and whispered, "Let's you and me sit with her today." And that's what they did, as soon as Sunday School was over.

"Good morning, Aunt Jane," whispered Susan.

Aunt Jane—Robbie and Sarah had always called Miss Bolton that, even though for years their neighbor would never speak to their mother! (Nobody would have believed then that the two ladies had once been best friends!) To Susan, and to everyone else in Braeburn district, she was Miss Jane Bolton, and nothing else. Unless they added things like Old High and Mighty. Or, Old Starchy. Or, Old Miss Flintstone. And, well, in a way, she *deserved* the nicknames.

This Sunday Sarah could feel Aunt Jane's arm trembling against her own. Aunt Jane was nervous. Sarah knew how she felt. Oh, she knew *exactly* how she felt! Because, one evening almost a year ago, Sarah had done in church what Aunt Jane meant to do. Testify—tell all the people what Jesus had done for her.

It's a hard thing to do, sometimes. But it's lovely when it's over, and everybody knows that you love Jesus and mean to follow Him. Sarah knew all about Aunt Jane's resolve, because it was exactly why she had come back west to Braeburn to live. To show everybody that Jesus had changed her. She *wasn't* Miss Flintstone anymore. Or Old This or That. She was a child of God!

About the time Brother Hammond usually began preaching, he stood looking down at the people. He was smiling happily. "Our sister Jane Bolton has asked to speak to us this morning," he said. "The time is yours, sister."

Aunt Jane got up and she told them. Oh, she told them! How sorry she was for the way she had lived all those years. How glad she was that Jesus Christ had changed her life. And the church was *quiet.* You could hear a single fly buzzing at one of the choir windows. Then people began wiping their eyes and blowing their noses softly. As soon as Aunt Jane sat down, Sister Hammond at the wheezy organ began playing "Amazing Grace." Father's tenor went floating out, clear and strong, over all the other voices.

Afterward, people came crowding to shake Aunt Jane's hand. And Mother introduced people to "my friend, Martha Chernishenko." She said it proudly. That was like Mother. She was friendly clear through.

Sarah was thinking of all that this morning as Wally rattled them along to school. She was proud of her mother. But all the same she was relieved that there were no Chernishenko children to go to school. Imagine having to be friendly to a lot of little "Rooshians" in school. How Grace Millar and some of the other big girls would tease!

They bossed the indoor work at school this morning. Grace was Teacher's sister-in-law, so she got to be Big Boss. Little girls, including Sarah and Susan, were sent to pump water, out in the yard. They carried it indoors by pailfuls. The big girls washed the blackboards and shoved the desks into one corner. Then all the little girls swept the floor. That was a dusty job.

After that the big girls stepped on top of desks and from there to windowsills to wash the tall windows and polish them. Then they washed and polished the desks, and the little girls scrubbed the floors—the schoolroom, the halls, the porch, and the porch steps. You had to be careful not to get slivers in your hands and knees.

When all was done, the school smelled of wetness, soap,

and polish. And everything was so clean and quiet it made you feel like a stranger in school.

Meanwhile Grant Millar, Teacher's husband, had been helping her to boss the boys' job outdoors. They raked the yard and built a big pile of trash for the bonfire. They straightened fences and the backstop, and mended the teeters and swings—whatever mending was necessary.

Then 3 o'clock came—bonfire time! Teacher rang the bell, and all the boys and girls came running. Some had potatoes or apples to roast. Some had only their leftover dinner sandwiches. A few had popcorn in wire poppers. But Teacher had made doughnuts for everybody, and a five-gallon can of lemonade.

Everyone sat around the fire. Their backs were slightly chilly, because it was so early in spring. But their faces got warmed; so did their hands and feet. Grant Millar told nature stories as long as the food was roasting. Afterward they sang themselves hoarse. They sang "Pictures in the clouds" and "Old Black Joe" and "Beautiful River" and "Darling Nellie Gray" and "My Bonnie Lies Over the Ocean." After the doughnuts and lemonade, Teacher made a speech. She thanked everybody for working so hard, cooperating so well, and doing such a good job of the cleanup. Then they all went home.

"Come home with me," Sarah coaxed Susan.

Susan wanted to, awfully. But she wasn't sure that her ma and pa would still be at the Scotts. And Susan was always dependable. She drove home with Chuckie and Bertie—but waved as they drove off, just to show how much she would have liked to go along with Sarah.

The Gerricks were still at the Scotts when Sarah and Robbie got home. So were the Chernishenkos. The kitchen was full of smells and working people when Sarah came in. Mr.

and Mrs. Chernishenko were rubbing salt into the big raw hams, and packing them into a large barrel. The hams would be stored in the cool woodshed until the salt had had time to penetrate. Then they'd be smoked.

The Chernishenkos walked away across the pasture to Aunt Jane's place. Aunt Jane had stayed till noon, Mother said. She still had to be careful not to tire herself too much.

"But those Rooshians sure can work," said Mr. Gerrick approvingly.

"Yes," said Father. "Jane is fortunate in her hired help this year." He never called the Chernishenkos *Rooshians*. They were Ukrainians.

The two men were making sausage in the sausage maker while Mrs. Scott and Mrs. Gerrick took jars and jars of hot canned meat out of a large, steaming boiler. Then they wiped off the greasy outsides, and set them aside to cool. Pails and crocks full of cracklings, lard, and headcheese crowded the kitchen table.

"Well, Sarah!" said Susan's ma. That meant, "Are you *still* standing around?" And it probably meant, "My Susan would have changed her dress by now, and begun to make herself useful."

Mother said, "Keith is doing all the milking tonight. You had better tend to the chicks and goslings and gather the eggs. But first of all, run down to the cellar for some vegetables. Hurry. We need them for supper. Help yourself to a drumstick if you're hungry."

"We had doughnuts and lemonade at school," Sarah called out as she ran down the cellar steps.

At first it seemed pitch-dark down there. Smells crowded up to meet her. Earthy smells and oily smells. The oil was from the incubator, with its 132 chicken eggs on a tray, and its long panel window. Through it you could see the thermometer resting on the eggs. The tiny lamp that heated the incubator gave off just enough light so you could see.

Another week and the eggs would crack open and a lot of wet, wobbly chicks would struggle out. As soon as they dried off, chicks became the cheepiest things! You couldn't *believe* all that noise and life could be locked up in those shells!

"Sarah? Are you coming?" called Mother. "Hurry!"

She jumped up and began piling vegetables into an old grape basket.

A while later, wearing her home dress, with an old, thick sweater of Robbie's over it, Sarah trotted out to the brooder house. It was a small, low place, next to the chicken house. The brooder was a large, shallow box, with a wide, umbrella hood of tin hanging over it. The area under the hood was heated by a tiny oil-burning stove.

The moment Sarah opened the door, 127 two-week-old chicks began shouting at her in unison: "Cheep-cheep-cheep!" Sarah hurried to fill the troughs with food and the jars with water. Then she made sure the stove was burning well.

The goslings, 18 of them, were in a box in the south corner of the brooder house. They were smart. They came pattering toward Sarah when she peered over the edge of the box. Their greeting was a soft *peelee-peelee* sound. Later, when they grew up, one goose would outshout all the chickens. But now they were soft and cuddly and easy to love.

Sarah brought young dandelion greens to them, handfuls of green grass, and a panful of boiled wheat. Then she went next door for the eggs. Most of them were cold. The hens had left their nests and were roosting on poles, groaning and complaining softly. But that was sham. Hens always sounded sad when they were contented.

The really sad creature was Ginger the cat. Suddenly Sarah felt Ginger's furry tail swishing around her ankles. Ginger was mewing and mewing, like a mother cat whose kittens have been taken from her. Sarah felt a lump in her throat. She picked Ginger up. The cat's forelegs went around her neck in a tight hug, but she still kept mewing.

"I haven't forgotten Spencer either," Sarah whispered. And she hadn't. It had been an interesting day, too busy a day for her to have much time for thinking private thoughts. But missing a friend is a deep thing. It goes on and on even when you think and speak of other things.

"But he was only a dog, after all!" she heard Susan's ma exclaim as Sarah entered the kitchen with the three-gallon pailful of tan-colored eggs.

Only a dog. Spencer! Suddenly Sarah felt as if her heart were crowding her chest.

The worst was when Mrs. Gerrick talked to Robbie later while he sat on the bench behind the table, waiting for supper. Sarah saw Mother glance anxiously at him. All the Scotts knew he must feel pretty bad. But he said nothing and remained sitting there. Father changed the subject, and everyone ate supper. Then the Gerricks drove home.

After dishes, and after the kitchen had been tidied up and the floor washed (Mother did most of that), Sarah ran up to her room. It was dark, but she knew where the matches were. She struck one carefully on the underside of the window-sill and lifted the flowery lamp shade and lit the lamp. Her fingers shook with excitement. She had just had the most tremendous idea!

Tomorrow was Tuesday. And ever since Teacher came to Braeburn, Tuesday was composition day. Sarah had brought her scribbler upstairs with her. She found a clean page and wrote the title of her story: MY FRIEND SPENCER.

She wrote—and wrote. About all the loving things Spencer used to do, and all the fun they had shared.

"Sarah! Sarah Naomi Scott!"

Sarah jumped at the sound of her mother's shocked voice, and her pen skittered across the page.

"Are you *still* up? It's past 10!" Mother's voice came up through the hole in the floor made for the stovepipe.

"Blow out that lamp. In a hurry!"

"Y-yes, Mother."

Pouf! Out it went. The composition was almost done, anyway. Sarah stretched her tired fingers and arms. She felt a lot better inside now.

CHAPTER 2

BOUNCER MAKES
A CHOICE

THE BELL RANG after the last recess the next afternoon and Braeburn School pupils came running back into the schoolroom. Out in the yard, so strangely neat today, the big girls and boys had been playing softball. The younger girls had been bouncing balls and skipping rope. Sarah was out of breath. She had been doing "Mabel, Mabel."

That skipping rhyme begins slow and easy, sort of sing songy:

> "Mabel, Mabel,
> Set the table.
> Don't forget the chairs . . ."

At first you have time to skip slowly. But then, watch out!

"Salt and PEPPER!" shriek all the girls. At "pepper" the turners whirl the rope like mad and you skip fast—until you miss—and are out. Sarah had counted up to 37 without missing—for the first time in her life—when the bell rang. That was too bad. Now she couldn't be sure who was the champion skipper in her grade. Veronica Siddons had gone to 38 once.

Teacher stood smiling at all the puffing, red-faced children who thumped in and slid into their seats. "I'm going to give you a change today—a treat," she said. "One of the compositions that was handed in is so good, I have to share it."

Bump, went Sarah's heart. And then she thought, *Oh, please. Not mine!* She tried to signal with her eyes. Robbie was here. He mustn't hear the story. But, sure enough, Teacher picked up Sarah's scribbler. She could tell it by the ink spot on the cover. Teacher began reading, "My Friend Spencer."

The composition told it all: Spencer the guardian. Spencer the watchman. Spencer the friend. Most of all, *the friend.* He loved—and loved—and loved.

Sarah couldn't look up. She couldn't look around. When someone suddenly stood up and walked out, she knew it must be Robbie, but she didn't see him go. Teacher stopped reading to stare at the shut door. She looked disturbed, but she didn't call Robbie back. A minute later there was the sound of a horse galloping away—Wally. And still Teacher read on— right down to the minute when Sarah and Robbie found their friend curled up in the harness room. And she told of the grave in the orchard.

Sarah's face was down on her desk, hidden in the crook of her arm. She could hear the little girls sobbing. Even some of the big ones blew their noses. It was the strangest thing.

Then it was over. "All right now. Let's get to work," Teacher said briskly. "Sarah, I'd like to see you for a moment after four." *

Oh dear! But whatever Teacher wanted to talk about, it couldn't be very dreadful. She was smiling when Sarah looked up. When all the others were starting for home, she said, "If

* School closed at 4 o'clock

you get a chance, Sarah, speak to Robbie for me. Tell him I would not have read that story aloud if I had known how it would affect him. By the way, we have a new litter of pups at our farm—"

"Robbie says he doesn't want a pup around," Sarah said sadly.

"Well, all the same—you gave me a great deal of pleasure. I believe you may be a writer some day. That will be all."

Any other day Sarah would have been half dizzy, hearing Teacher say that. Today she was too disturbed. She kept her eyes open for Robbie as she rode home. He wouldn't have gone home. She was fairly certain of that. He'd have had to *explain.*

She saw a horse and a rider coming over a long hill to the south. That was the land Keith had bought. It would become part of his horse-raising farm. The horse tossed his head just the way Wally always did. It *was* Wally, with Robbie on his back.

He joined Sarah. Neither of them said a word, but they rode on home together, just as usual. Robbie looked sort of ordinary too. He was different though—quieter. In the days and weeks that followed, he never mentioned Spencer. He went hiking a lot in the woods when his chores were done, but he'd always liked to do that. Usually he'd had Spencer leaping alongside or pacing right beside him. (Spencer always knew instantly if you were glad or sad. And the way you felt was the way he acted.)

The day Sarah was stopped by Grant Millar, Teacher's new husband, Robbie had stayed at home to do fieldwork.

Grant Millar was a shy man. He seldom spoke to anyone unless they spoke to him first, so this was unusual. But ever since the day Braeburn heard him tell one of his nature stories—because Teacher coaxed him to—Sarah had a strong liking for him.

He was putting in a new fence along the roadway, digging holes, dropping in posts, and stringing the barbed wire taut. Grant Millar was one of the best livestock farmers in the district. That's what people said. Having a good fence was an important part of being a good livestock farmer.

When Sarah came riding, he left his work, and waited for her beside the road. "I hear that brother of yours wants a puppy," he said.

"Robbie? He doesn't" said Sarah gloomily.

"He does." Mr. Millar's eyes smiled. "He may not know it yet, but he does. Now, I happen to have a beautiful litter. The problem is how to get boy and dog together."

"It wouldn't work," said Sarah decidedly. After all, she knew Robbie.

"It's worth a try," said the farmer, sounding stubborn in a friendly way. "Your Spencer, as it happens, was a grandsire of this litter. One is his spitting image. I'd depend on him to win his way into Robbie's heart, given the chance."

"If it could be sort of *accidental*," said Sarah, with just a glimmer of hope. "But how?"

"Let's put on our thinking caps," said Grant Millar. He gave Blackie a friendly slap. She had been snuffling his face and hands and overalls. All animals liked Grant Millar. He raised his cap politely to Sarah and went back to his work on the fence.

Sarah had forgotten all about their talk a few days later when Father said they had better take Wally and the buggy to school. For once she was glad to leave Blackie at home. It was a dismal morning. Rain had fallen all night. She knew now mucky the road would be. And cleaning mud off Blackie was not one of Sarah's favorite chores.

"And as long as you're using the buggy," remarked Father, "you might as well call at Grant Millar's. He offered me several bushels of that new variety of No. 1 Northern wheat to try this spring. I told him you'd stop by for it."

Even then Sarah didn't suspect a thing.

It drizzled all day, and Sarah felt grumpy about having to drive two extra miles in this weather. Her coat was damp. The blanket that was draped over her knees was damp. The road was squishy with mud, and Wally kept flinging blobs of it into her lap. Some of it smudged one edge of her reader. And if there was one thing that made Sarah cross, it was having her books messed up.

Mr. Millar's granary door stood open. He stuck his head out into the rain. "Oh, it's you," he said. "Give me a hand with these sacks, will you, Robbie?"

That moment an exciting thought struck Sarah. *Let's put on our thinking caps,* he'd said. What if Father and he—What if the puppies were in the granary!

She tumbled out of the buggy and tied the reins to the nearest fencepost. Then she squished toward the granary. Impatiently, she looked over the farmer and several sacks of wheat and Robbie stooping to pick up a sack. Beyond him was a shallow box with a heap of coats and sacks in it. And on them lay a huddle of dogs—a mother and her pups.

One was sitting up, looking at Robbie. And Robbie was staring back at him—just staring.

Sarah gave a happy squeal and ran across to kneel on the rough floor, all dusty from the grain.

"Look! It's Spencer! He's just like Spencer! See his white chest. And the spot on this ear and his white feet. Oh, you're the cutest thing!"

She was patting the fat furry pup. And he licked her hand. Then he bounced out of the box and went bouncing over the floor to sit, looking up at Robbie, waving his ridiculous stump of a tail.

Happily, Sarah looked past them at Grant Millar. He gave her a slow wink. But Robbie pushed the puppy aside gently and stooped again to pick up the sack.

"Here, I'll give you a hand with that," said Millar.

Two plump sackfuls of wheat filled the box behind the seat. One rested heavily on Sarah and Robbie's feet.

"The pup is yours if you'd like him," remarked the farmer as he stepped back from storing the last of the wheat. "I have no need for so many dogs, you know."

"Oh, Mr. Millar!" said Sarah.

"Thanks all the same," said Robbie. "Tch, tch. Get up, Wally."

Robbie made such a short turn that the wheels grated against the buggy box. Mud and water dripped from the wheels, and Wally's hooves made sucking, squishing sounds as they drove down the lane. Behind them a howl arose. Startled, Robbie reined Wally to a stop. There, in the lake of mud, sat a chubby puppy. When they stopped he began yipping happily and ran to catch up.

Sarah scrambled over the wheels. She didn't care what Robbie said or thought now. She got messed up, all of her, but that didn't matter either.

"You poor thing! You poor thing!" crooned Sarah. She picked him up, and he wriggled with joy.

"What do you think you're going to do with him?" said Robbie.

"I'm taking him home, so there! Mr. Millar said we could, and I'm going to. If you don't want him, I do."

But the pup knew whose puppy he really was. Sarah tucked a bit of the blanket around him and he didn't mind that. But he burrowed under it until he rested against Robbie's shin, and he went to sleep there.

Sarah didn't mind. A grin was growing inside her and

beaming from her eyes. She had to suck in her cheeks to keep it from cracking her face—for Robbie's sake.

One thing bothered her though. How could kind Mr. Millar have let the puppy get away, out into all that drizzle and mud? What if the pup had been lost? What if he'd been badly chilled? The next time she had a chance, she stopped to ask him.

"It wouldn't have been for long," Mr. Millar said. "I would have seen to that, of course. But you see, when a dog has found his man, he has the right to follow him." The farmer had a twinkle in his eyes. "I could depend on his penetrating howl."

When they brought him home that first day, Sarah gathered the bedraggled puppy in her arms, along with her lunch pail and books and scribblers. Everything was about equally muddy by then.

"Sarah! *What* in the *world!*" began Mother when Sarah and her armload appeared in the kitchen doorway. Then, "Tell us what happened," Mother continued in a quieter, interested way.

She let the pup go bouncing across the clean kitchen floor, leaving black rosettes wherever his paws had been. He bounced up to Father, where he sat beside the table, and licked his ankles. He bounced up to Mother, and stood to put his front paws on her apron. He bounced back to Sarah, who still stood laughing on the rug near the door. He rolled on her muddy rubbers.

"I guess we'd better call him Bouncer," said Sarah, as she tickled his fat, muddy stomach.

And Bouncer was his name from that day.

During the day, he was a happy-go-lucky puppy. He had probably never taken milk from a pan. Sarah let him lick milk from her fingers once. After that he knew precisely what to do. He had probably never had a bath before, except a washing by his mother's tongue. He allowed Sarah to soap him while Father held him in the warm water to calm him.

He grew frisky again when she patted him dry and began rubbing and fluffing his fur. But when Robbie came indoors for supper, Bouncer forgot everything else. He was Robbie's dog. The question was, would Robbie consent to be his boy?

For a wonder Mother allowed Sarah to make up a bed for Bouncer behind the kitchen stove. Mrs. Scott was not fond of having pets indoors.

"Tuck the old alarm clock in with him," Father said.

"You're joking, Father!" said Sarah.

"No. I mean it. Bouncer is used to sleeping close to his mother and hearing her heart thud. The clock will make him feel at home until he gets used to us."

It seemed to work. Bouncer snuggled down and snoozed quietly all through the evening while Sarah and Robbie and Stuart studied around the kitchen table. Then came family devotions and bedtime.

That night Sarah's dreams were busy. She seemed to be going down a muddy road in the dark. She could hear Bouncer howling and yelping. She tried desperately to go to him, but her feet got heavier and heavier with mud, and finally she couldn't even lift them. She was stuck! She tried to call, but only a squeak came out. Then his howls died away, and she was afraid he was lost for good, out in the chill night. And she was alone in the dark—all alone.

"Sarah!" Someone quite close whispered her name. She opened her eyes. It was morning! The sun shone through her two windows, but it was early, early. Her big brother Stuart was peeking in through the door. He made hushing motions as he whispered, "Come, see."

Something unusual must be happening. He looked happy and amused.

Stuart was special. Sarah's oldest brother, Keith, was more fun in a way. He was exciting. Handsome! He could tell many stories about the years when he was a cowboy out west. And Robbie—well, he was closest to her own age, and they teased each other a lot. They disagreed often, but they were pals. Stuart was the one who listened quietly to her troubles. And he was smart! This spring he would finish high school in Blakely. Hardly any farm boys went that far in school!

So when he motioned to her, Sarah slipped out of bed, and went barefoot behind him. Carefully, because some of the steps creaked. In the kitchen, Stuart pointed. There sat Robbie on the floor beside the cookstove, asleep. His feet stretched out in front of him. He had put on an old sweater of Father's over his pajamas, and buttoned it up. A furry head poked over the sagging neckline. Bouncer. He was snoozing too.

Sarah and Stuart tiptoed softly upstairs again. Sarah was shivering and laughing silently. "How did you find out?" she whispered.

"Well, for one, the pup quit yelping. Then I noticed Robbie's bed was empty. So I went down to investigate. Robbie is caught. The pup has won his heart for sure."

Just then they heard a creak. Robbie was coming. He started when he saw them, then he grinned sheepishly. "Some beggar," he said. "This is sure some beggar." Bouncer was still in his arms.

"What'll Mother say?" said Sarah. Taking pets to your bedroom was worse than having them in the kitchen.

"I think she'll settle for some silence this morning," said Stuart. "Get back to bed, Sis. It's only 5 o'clock."

That evening Sarah and her parents stood at the kitchen window, watching Robbie and Bouncer go toward the barn. "Well, Sheila," said Father. "It's a boy and his dog again."

"I can't see why he had to be so stubborn about getting a

pup in the first place," said Mother, sounding exasperated.

"He resisted learning one of life's lessons, is all," said Father. "He thought that to open his heart to a new love was to be a traitor to the old. But love is expandable. Do you know what I'm talking about, Sarah?"

"Yes. No. I don't know."

He laughed. "And that's an honest answer, I have no doubt, Princess Sarah."

"Time to feed those chicks and goslings," said Mother crisply. "Run along, Sarah."

The brooder house was twice as noisy tonight as it was a few weeks ago. Since the second incubatorful of eggs hatched, there were twice as many mouths to shout, "Cheep! Cheep! Cheep!" at Sarah.

"Cheep, yourself!" said Sarah. "Kur-r-r-r-r!" (That's BE STILL! in mother hen language.)

It was funny. Instant quiet came. Only the goslings kept murmuring "peelee-peelee." But then the noise started all over again, until Sarah had filled the long feeding troughs and watering jars.

You couldn't simply set shallow pans full of water out for the chicks. They would hop right in, get wet all over, get chilled—and probably die. Chicks die easy! So you filled a glass jar with water and clapped a saucer over the mouth, then turned the whole thing upside down—fast. Only a little water came seeping out. A ring of fluffy black chicks gathered around each saucer and dipped in their tiny yellow beaks, and raised them to let the water trickle down their throats.

Yet chicks knew many things by instinct. No mother hens were around to scold some sense into them. But they knew without being told. How to drink, how to scratch for food, how to crouch down and keep perfectly still when danger threatened. They went into the crouching act now—and there was Ginger, peering at them over the rim of the brooder box. She must look like an immense orange beast to them, a fearsome tiger, maybe.

"Meow?" she asked sadly.

"Sure. Just about through," said Sarah.

Poor Ginger. She still missed Spencer dreadfully. Now that Robbie had accepted Bouncer, Ginger was the only one who couldn't be comforted. She didn't even have any kittens to cuff and lick and teach how to go mouse hunting.

But that night Ginger surprised everyone. Robbie and Sarah had made a bed for Bouncer in the barn. Mother said firmly that if the pup meant to howl anyway, he might as well do it away from the house. They wound up the clock and tucked it in beside Bouncer, but he whimpered.

Then Ginger peered over the box, purring. She jumped in and lay down beside Bouncer, tucking three paws under her, the way cats do. But she put fourth leg over Bouncer's neck, and touched the closest ear with her tongue. The ear twitched. She waved her tail and blinked at Sarah.

"You may go. Everything's under control. *I'll* take care of *this* crybaby," she seemed to be saying.

Bouncer had come home.

CHAPTER 3

AN ARRIVAL
AND A MYSTERY

SARAH STOOD looking out the window. She felt grumpy. It was raining. Again. Today she and Robbie would have to take Wally and the buggy to school once more. "What's the use of having a pony," she grumbled, "if you can't *ride* her?"

"If it keeps on raining, you'll *have* to take Blackie out, if only for the excercise," Mother warned. "You don't want her to get out of condition."

Just then Father came in and stood dripping on the kitchen rug. Rain trickled from his hair and ran down his mackitosh.

"A million-dollar rain," he said, mopping his hair with a large red hanky. "Cheer up, Princess. Maybe *this* year we'll be able to buy that car."

Wow! That moment the sun burst out in Sarah's private skies. A car! Almost every other family in Braeburn owned one. Always, Father had said the Scotts couldn't afford one. Not yet. They had land and machinery debts to pay. And debts came first.

When Wally trotted up to the gate, Sarah ran outdoors

quite cheerfully. She had a woollen blanket draped over her head. They had cowhides to sit on and to cover their knees.

"Giddap!" said Robbie, and they were off.

Dismal howls came floating out of the toolshed. Bouncer always had to be shut in until Robbie was gone.

The rain came beating down as they faced the north wind while driving down the lane. Sarah was glad when they turned west. She could pull the edge of the blanket forward, and shield her face. Robbie guided Wally onto the grassy strip that ran along the road. Here you could hear only the dull thud of hooves on the soft carpet of green. The wheels turned almost soundlessly. The rain had made the wood swell so eveything on the buggy was tight and it couldn't rattle.

Millions of yellow dandelions, buttercups, and purple crocuses buttoned the grass to the earth here. Along the fence grew pincherry and chokecherry and saskatoon berry bushes —all in bloom. Breathing the air was almost like drinking perfume.

"And Father says this year, maybe, we'll buy a car," chattered Sarah.

They argued a bit about what kind of car they'd like. Sarah said she'd beg for a shiny sedan with glass windows all around. Like Aunt Jane's. But Robbie said they'd buy the car they could afford. *If* they could afford any at all.

Rainy weather wasn't talking weather. Rain pelted down on them, and Sarah could feel the cold wet soaking through the blanket now. Any minute it would begin trickling down her neck. But Robbie didn't seem to mind. His hands were bare.

In fact, Robbie didn't seem to mind *anything*, thought Sarah impatiently. Except Spencer's death. He didn't mind that they were still driving a buggy when *everybody* had a car. He didn't mind if people teased him, so he was no fun to tease—

Well, there were a few things he minded—like milking cows and drying dishes. And he did mind if anybody was hurt. In school he always defended the little boys if the big ones bothered them. That was something to be proud of.

By the time Wally turned into the Braeburn yard, Sarah had cheered herself up, in spite of the sopping blanket. Her hair was in tight curls all over her head, so all of Mother's brushing was useless. The back of her gingham dress was soaked too. But Mother wasn't here to see that.

Sarah took the first chance to whisper her exciting secret to Susan Gerrick: "This year, maybe we'll buy a car! Father said so!"

School smelled of wet wool and rubbers and chalk this morning. During recess, half the pupils played blackboard games, like Cat and hangman and building squares. The rest were in the basement, playing Magic Broomstick. Or jumping down the stairs. Or, they were swinging on the rafters. Or playing leapfrog. It was dark and noisy down there. Teacher cut recesses short and spent a longer time reading to the school than she usually did. The book was LORNA DOONE.

It was an exciting story, but it was an "I" story. Sarah got impatient with "I" stories, mostly. They either sounded braggy or stupid. This one sounded sort of stupid. It was about Master John Ridd, who was big for his age and sort of clumsy. But Lorna Doone was *beautiful* and she *liked* Master John!

Last year, thought Sarah—Last year, when she was a lot younger, she had been mad at Herbie Gerrick for wanting to marry Kathleen, her big sister. It seemed funny now. Kathleen had always said she'd marry somebody really important some day. And Herbie—well, Herbie seemed like a nobody to Sarah. Just plain Herbie Gerrick! He was a farmer, and that was all right. Look at Father! He was a farmer too, and Sunday School superintendent, with a lovely tenor voice.

Now, Herbie Gerrick was going to be a minister! That was a Somebody! He didn't decide to be a minister in order to be a Somebody. God simply told him to be one! He loved his farm and his horses. He had built a lot of nifty cupboards in the house, where he and Kathleen had hoped to live. God told him to sell it all, so he did. Now Keith had bought the place.

"Sarah? Sarah Naomi Scott, where are you?" called Teacher. "Daydreaming again?"

Sarah started. Everybody was looking at her, and some were laughing. Teacher had finished the chapter in LORNA DOONE, and all the classes were working at their spelling now—all but Sarah.

The sun came out during the afternoon, and driving home was lovely. A surprise waited for Sarah at home. Aunt Jane had come to visit, not in her car. She had *walked,* across the pasture. It was a whole half mile, and she had used her cane! She was sitting in the living room, having tea, when Sarah came home. Her eyes sparkled. Her cheeks were pink. She was almost pretty.

"I've never, absolutely never, enjoyed a walk so much," Sarah heard her say. "Sheila, the air is simply—simply intoxicating. All the fence rows in bloom like that." She saw Sarah smile, and added, "Isn't it beautiful?"

"It's like drinking perfume," said Sarah.

The ladies laughed. Then Sarah ran upstairs to change her dress. She could still hear their voices. Mother said that Aunt Jane must stay for supper, and Aunt Jane said, all right, she would. Then Mother asked if Aunt Jane had seen Mabel Slocum lately. (That was the Scott's nearest neighbor, the big jolly lady with the flyaway hair and the booming voice.) And Aunt Jane said, no, not lately.

"I'm worried about her," said Mother.

Sarah didn't wait to hear any more. She ran down and out, to do her chores. But first she visited Blackie, who was lonesome after being in the barn all day. Sarah promised to take her for a ride later—if there was time. Then she raced for the brooder house.

Chores were part of living on a farm. They were good and not so good. Everybody had chores to do, and nobody did them for you unless you were sick. That was good because it showed that you were important. Father and Mother and the boys *depended* on you. It wasn't so good when you felt like doing something else, for a change. The chores were there. You had to stick with them. Dependability—that was one of Father's favorite words.

This spring Sarah did not have to do any milking. But she had to feed the chicks and goslings. She had to gather the eggs in baskets and pack them in crates so they were ready for Father to take to Blakely. She had to help Robbie feed the calves, and she had to wash the milk pails every evening.

Robbie had his have-tos too. When there was company for supper and Mother could not do her share of the milking, he had to. But then Sarah had to fill the woodbox in Robbie's place. Like today.

Bouncer was a darling and a nuisance when she was stacking wood on the little coaster wagon and trying to pull it from the woodpile to the kitchen door. His tongue swiped at her face and hands and ankles. He trotted before her and beside her. He rolled right where she wanted to step. Sarah laughed and scolded.

Ginger was no use either. She sat looking at Bouncer, waving her tail, and blinking up at Sarah. "Isn't he smart?" she seemed to be saying.

Ginger reminded her of Susan Gerrick's Ma, who was

always bragging about how *capable* Susan was. And she *was*. She could bake and ice cakes without help from her ma, though she wasn't 11 years old yet.

Thump went the last armload of wood into the woodbox. Finished. All her before-supper chores were done. She couldn't feed the calves and wash the pails until after the milk had been run through the separator. Maybe she'd have time to go for a run on Blackie before supper—

But that minute Father came in with two pails of milk, and Mother asked Sarah to set the table. Father poured the milk through a sieve into the tank at the top of the separator. Then he began turning the handle, fast and faster. When he reached 60 turns per minute the machine settled down to a steady hum. That was the time to turn on the faucet. A broad stream of skim milk came out of the wider spout and ran into the pail. A thin yellowish-pinkish thread of cream spun from the other spout into a gallon crock.

Father's head and shoulders bobbed 60 times a minute when he asked Aunt Jane, "How are the Chernishenkos working out? Everything satisfactory, I hope?"

"Y-yes," said Aunt Jane.

"Anything wrong?" Sarah knew Father would feel responsible if something *was* wrong. He had hired the Ukrainian farmer for Aunt Jane. "Not lazy, are they?"

"Oh, no," she said, looking a trifle worried. "But have you noticed something secretive, almost *furtive* about them?"

Just then Robbie came in with another pail of milk. "Don't you agree, Robbie?" she said. "You were there in the barn last night when I went to talk with Mr. Chernishenko. Didn't you get the feeling he was trying to hide something from me?"

Sarah was counting people and setting out plates when something suddenly occurred to her. She glanced at Robbie in astonishment. *Last night Robbie didn't go to Aunt Jane's at all.* Usually he did, just in case Mr. Chernishenko and Aunt Jane needed help. But last evening she and Robbie had played ball out in the yard after supper, with Bouncer to help—or hinder—at fielding. He *thought* he was helping!

In the middle of the game, Robbie exclaimed, "Oh, dear!" He'd clean forgotten to go to Aunt Jane's. Then he added, "Guess it's too late now." And it was. For that minute Father had called them in for family devotions. After that they did their homework, then went to bed. So.

Robbie glanced at Aunt Jane in an interested way, but he didn't look at Sarah.

After supper Stuart took Aunt Jane home. Father sat in the corner armchair while Mother washed the dishes and Sarah dried them.

"You *do* think the Chernishenkos are all right, don't you?" Mother asked Father.

"Of course. Don't worry. Probably just a case of Old World prejudice against taking orders from a woman. It takes a while for Europeans to get used to our Canadian ways."

When she was free to go, Sarah raced outdoors to give Blackie a run. They used the pasture, because there was no mud there. Blackie raced round and round, and all the colts and calves got excited and began racing around too. Then Bouncer joined them, and all the geese honked and screeched. It was a wild, mad, noisy ride.

Father and Mother came out and stood at the corral gate, laughing. But not for long. "Don't forget to wash the milk pails," called Mother.

Sarah turned Blackie back to the barn. Twice she had forgotten to do the pails. Once Mother did them for her—but the next time Sarah had to get out of bed when all the rest had gone to bed. With only the clock and one lonesome-

looking lamp for company, she'd had to *wash those pails.* Because that was her job.

The weather next day was fine, so both Sarah and Robbie rode to school. Blackie swooped along, smooth as a swallow's flight. But Wally— Sarah knew just what it felt like to go bumping and humping along on his back.

On the way home she was daydreaming again—Keith, her oldest brother, had left for Alberta last week. He was bringing a bunch of fillies and mares home to start his horse ranch. What if he'd bring a pony for Robbie? She would feel so much better if Robbie had a better horse to ride. She often felt guilty. Selfish. Daydreams didn't often come true, she knew. But it would be nice—

"Hey!" Robbie pulled Wally to a stop. "Look—out that way!" He was pointing southeast.

Over the rim of hills came a bunch of horses, with one rider hazing them along.

"Keith!" yelled Robbie. "Yippie!" He was off on lumbering Wally. But Wally could cover ground faster than you'd think. Robbie, riding bareback as always, practically stretched out on Wally's back, coaxing him to go faster. But they couldn't outdistance Blackie.

They were in the meadow now and had to watch for gopher holes. Robbie and Sarah slowed. The band was closer now, and the distant rider raised his hat and swung it around. Keith. On Masquerade, his trick pony!

"Yippie!" yelled Sarah and Robbie together, and they were off at gallop. They shouldn't. They knew they shouldn't gallop here. But nothing happened. Except that Keith came flying to meet them.

"Hi, there, you two!" he called. He was proud and pleased with his band of horses. "I can use a couple of hazers."

So they helped him herd the band across the creek and over

the next hill and through the pasture gate and across to Keith's corral. The horses had come home, though they didn't know it yet.

Masquerade nickered at Blackie and Wally. They were familiar friends by now. But the new horses milled around, snorting, their heads up. One caught Robbie's eye. "Boy! Look at that bay!" he said.

"Like him?" said Keith.

"Boy!" Robbie sighed. "Some looker."

And he was handsome. Wally looked awfully clumsy beside him.

"What's his name?"

"Uh—that hasn't been decided yet," said Keith. "But, near as I can tell, his disposition matches his looks. Good mouth, good gait, good heart of courage." Keith often talked about horses almost as if they were people.

He needed Robbie's help for a bit more, so Sarah rode home alone. All the chores were waiting to be done, and she'd get a late start as it was. But she didn't ride straight home, all the same. While passing Aunt Jane's place, she could see the large neat garden with someone working in it. Mrs. Chernishenko.

Sarah remembered with a little guilty feeling that she had never really thanked the lady for the fancy Easter egg. It still lay in its nest of purple paper straw, in the old Murray sideboard in the kitchen. The few times Sarah had met Mrs. Chernishenko there were grown-ups around. If you were 11, you didn't interrupt grown-up conversation! But the longer you waited to say thank-you the harder it was.

Sarah decided to do it now, and have it *done*. It needn't take long.

At the gate she slid off Blackie's back, and tethered her to a post. She ran around Aunt Jane's house, and out to the

garden. But it was empty! There lay the hoe Mrs. Chernishenko had been using a moment ago. A row of plum trees, all
in bloom, hid the hired man's house. On the far side of the
trees, something dark moved quickly along. Ah, Mrs.
Chernishenko. Sarah ran after her.

The Chernishenko's house had a tall caragana hedge, like a
wall, around it with a gap in it for a gate. When Sarah came
through the gap, she saw Mrs. Chernishenko peering through
the hedge, and breathing hard. "H-hello, Mrs. Chernishenko,"
Sarah said in a small voice.

The lady whirled around. You wouldn't think such a large
lady could turn so fast. She moved quickly to the house door
and stood there. "What do you want?" she asked. "Is not goot
think you do, to fright me."

Sarah wanted to explain. But she was startled. She turned
and ran away as fast as she had come. She was just about to
ride off when Aunt Jane called from the steps of the big
house: "Anything wrong, Sarah?"

Now, it's funny. You may be just a bit angry, but as long as
you don't make anything of it, you can forget it quickly. But
when you begin telling on someone, you simply boil over.
That's what happened to Sarah.

Aunt Jane sighed. "There's something odd about that
woman," she said, looking worried. "If it's any comfort to you,
Sarah, she behaves the same way with me. She is friendly
enough when she comes to my house to help with the work
here. But I've never been allowed to set foot inside their house
since they moved in. Perhaps it's not in their tradition. I don't
know." She shrugged her shoulder and went indoors.

Sarah made up her mind as she rode home that she wasn't
going to say anything to anyone about Mrs. Chernishenko.
Mother would worry if she knew. So she gave Blackie a good
rubbing down and turned her into the pasture. She fed and

watered the chicks and goslings. She gathered the eggs. And because Robbie was going to be late, she even volunteered to fill the woodbox for him. And *then*, when she had been so kind and everything, then he had to take sides against her. Right at the supper table too!

"What did you do to Mrs. Chernishenko?" he said.

Sarah was so astonished, that she sat there with her mouth open. Maybe she looked guilty.

"You made her cry," added Robbie.

"Sarah Scott! Whatever—" began Mother.

Sarah boiled right over. "I didn't! I didn't say a single *word* to her. Except to say hello. I wanted to talk. I wanted to say thank-you for the egg."

She told the whole story exactly the way it happened. Father believed her. Maybe Mother did too, but she looked troubled. And Keith—Keith *always* took Sarah's side. Well, usually. Sarah had been so happy to have him home again. But Robbie had to go and spoil things.

"Well, if nothing happened, and if you didn't do or say anything, why did she have to go and send you a peace-offering again?" he asked.

"What did she send?" Mother wanted to know.

Robbie stuck his hand in his pocket and pulled out his red-spotted handkerchief, all balled up. Inside was another beautiful, painted egg.

"I don't *want* her egg," said Sarah. "She can just keep it! The other one too."

"Sarah, Sarah," Mother said.

Sarah felt like crying, but her heart was crowding her chest. It felt fiery hot. It wasn't fair to be scolded for nothing!

After supper she ran to sit on the corral gate. Robbie would call her when it was time to feed the calves. They were such sillies, with their little bunting horns, that he couldn't manage them alone. But it was Stuart who came to sit beside her.

Sarah sighed. Then she looked at Stuart, and he looked at her and smiled.

"They shouldn't blame me for something I never did," she burst out.

"No," agreed Stuart quietly.

"It's not *fair*. They're *always* blaming me for things!"

"Are they?" said Stuart. He was still smiling.

"Well, *sometimes*. And it makes me *so mad*."

After a little silence Stuart said, "It might help to remember how Jesus got blamed. For all the sins of the world. For mine."

"And mine," said Sarah in a small voice. "And He was quiet, wasn't He?"

"And forgiving—and loving," said Stuart.

They sat a while quietly, just thinking about that. When Robbie called, Stuart gave her a hand so she could jump clear to the ground in one jump.

CHAPTER 4

UNEXPECTED HAPPENINGS

A FEW DAYS later, Aunt Jane appeared in the Scott yard unexpectedly. At breakfast time! Her car came purring up the lane just a moment after Sarah spied Keith, riding up on Masquerade and leading that handsome new horse Robbie had admired.

Keith lived in his own house most of the time now, "batching," but he often dropped in for meals. He never came for all day unless Father asked him to help at a special farm job. Sawing wood, maybe, or cleaning out the well or chopping feed grain.

Sarah was always happy to see him. He was fun and exciting. And here he was with that new horse. But it was breakfast time, and she had to hurry because it was a school day. Besides, Aunt Jane was coming in, and Sarah couldn't be rude and simply run past her. It was too bad things happened in a pile like this. For, of course, Sarah really liked to have Aunt Jane call. They had been friends for a long time.

"Well, good morning, good morning," said Aunt Jane. "How is everybody?"

"Well, *you* sound jaunty," said Father. "Sit down and have breakfast with us."

"Thank you, Sheila, John. But I can't face food so early in the day. Is that Keith I see tethering horses at the gate?" She peered through the kitchen window. "A handsome brute, I must say. Oh, don't look so startled, Sheila. I mean that young horse, not your son. Hmmm—If you'll excuse me—" And she walked right out again!

Mother laughed. "That's Jane for you," she said. "We might as well *all* have a look at the wonderful 'brute.' Yes, yes, Sarah—Robbie."

They were out like two shots.

There in the warm sun stood this young "brute." His head was up, but he stood quietly.

"Looks intelligent," said Father.

Keith laughed. "Looks aren't everything." And Sarah knew he must be thinking of Masquerade, who wasn't much to look at, but he was about as smart as a human being. And *smarter* in some things than people. He and Keith were friends the way Robbie and Spencer used to be.

Bouncer wasn't ready to take Spencer's place, but he was trying. As usual he crowded as close to Robbie's feet as possible. But Robbie had taken the new horse's bridle and was stroking the silky red-brown neck and velvety nose. The horse snuffed gently at Robbie's shoulders and ears and chest.

"Like him?" said Aunt Jane. Her eyes sparkled, and her cheeks were pink.

A little trembling thrill went through Sarah from head to toes. She knew—she knew what was coming.

"He's yours, Robbie," said Aunt Jane.

"Jane. Why, Jane!" said Mother.

"No, Jane," said Father, in a this-is-too-much tone.

But Robbie didn't say a word. He didn't even look at her while she explained how she got Keith to promise not to tell that he was to be on the lookout in Alberta for a special riding horse for Robbie. He just stood still and let the horse nuzzle him. But Sarah saw his legs trembling!

"Try him," Aunt Jane urged.

When he turned, his face was white under the spring tan. But he got into the saddle—a lovely tooled leather—and he laughed, but he was pretty close to crying. He turned the horse's head, and they were off.

"Beautiful! Beautiful!" murmured Aunt Jane.

"Lovely gait," said Father.

"Jane, you shouldn't have," protested Mother.

"Nonsense!" Aunt Jane always knew her own mind. "Who has a better right to a gift from me than Robbie? Consider how he loathes milking—yet how faithfully and uncomplainingly he took care of my stock—for how long—when I was in the hospital last fall! No, Sheila, I don't want to hear another word about it."

Father laughed, but his eyes were moist as he watched Robbie and the horse come tearing up the driveway. When Robbie threw himself off, he looked like a new boy. But he still didn't speak. He just looked at Aunt Jane.

She patted his shoulder. "There, there. Remember he's all yours." Then she drove away.

Bouncer was crowding Robbie's feet again, so he picked up the fat pup. Bouncer put out a timid tongue and licked the horse's nose. The horse threw up his head with a snort, but then he reached down and nuzzled the pup. The whole family laughed. Then everyone went indoors for breakfast.

After he had eaten, Robbie did a peculiar thing. He took the saddle off his horse and turned him into the corral. And he rode away, bareback, on *Wally!*

"Why?" whispered Sarah to Mother when she saw what Robbie meant to do.

"It's too big a joy for him to take in so suddenly," said Mother, with a serious smile. "That's my guess." And Mother probably was right. She usually was about Robbie. "Some joys can be almost too big and shining for us to accept—especially if they're unexpected."

Riding to school with Robbie, Sarah grinned until her cheeks ached. And Robbie's eyes shone. They thought of names for the horse. Some were silly, some stupid. Robbie was going to have more trouble deciding on a name than she had with Blackie.

"Why don't you call your horse Bayard?" Sarah said.

"Bayard—" said Robbie. "How did you think of that?"

"I don't know. It just popped into my head. I read it somewhere, I guess. He's a bay, so—"

"Bayard was the name of a magical horse in a book that was written hundreds of years ago," Robbie said.

They talked about names again on the way home. It had been a hot day. Ahead of them, in the east, a blackish-bluish cloud was rapidly blotting out the sky. It got bigger and bigger, a monster balloon, with a growl in its throat, and a queer jagged line of white teeth in the middle.

"Look at that funny white streak," said Sarah.

"Funny! That's hail! Come on, Sarah. We'd better fly."

So they flew. Wally and Blackie were both nervous. They snorted as they pounded along. Wind gusts began to hit them. And lightning zig-zagged across the cloud and played tag with the earth here and there.

"We've got to find shelter," yelled Robbie. "No, no! Not that haystack! If it's struck, it will burn. And not a tall tree. A low building—"

They both saw the ramshackly shed on the Heathe field.

The wire gate was down, so without discussion, they urged their horses toward the shack. Only two walls were standing, and the roof sagged. It leaked too, but a poor shelter was better than none.

By now white hail balls were batting down from the sky. They bounced around in huge leaps. In fact, the air was *full* of leaping balls. They clattered on the shingly roof that sheltered two horses and two breathless riders. Many of them bounded right in, hitting cheek or head or ankles, hard.

"Ouch!" screeched Sarah. "Each ball bounces three times. See? Ow-eech!"

Trying to talk was no use. All the world was one big roaring, crashing, rumbling noise. As Sarah and Robbie watched, the rolling green hills turned black, then white. They saw green trees stripped of their spring look. It was horrible and frightening.

In about 25 minutes, the storm was over, and the sun came out. It could come out—and smile down on them—when the whole world was killed!

Sarah shook as she led Blackie out of the shed and mounted. The air smelled of crushed grass and poplar leaves—green and bitter and sharp. The grassy trail that led to the road was deep in ice balls. The hail slid and crunched under the horses' hooves. And the wheat—all the wide rolling fields of young wheat was beaten to the ground.

"We-we're not going to b-buy th-that car this y-year," said Sarah with a catch in her throat.

"*Car!*" muttered Robbie. "Where's Father going to get the money to buy wheat seed to seed all the land again, that's what I wonder."

The sun smiled and the earth lay hushed. Except for the black mass hurrying westward, there wasn't a cloud in the sky. Not a bird warbled. The only sound was the crunch-

crunch under Blackie and Wally's hooves. They had to ride carefully so the horses would not stumble.

"Not on the grass!" said Robbie sharply. "Too slippery."

"What grass?" said Sarah dismally.

"Look! Look at Slocums'!" Robbie exclaimed.

They reined in their horses, to stare. To their left, lay green, green fields. Hardly any hail had fallen on this quarter of land.

When they reached home, Father was crossing the yard with two big pails of useless hail balls.

"Well!" he said, setting them down. "So you are unhurt. Thank God for that. Your mother was worried."

The house door slammed, and Mother came running out. "Where *were* you during the storm? One good thing, you had Wally and not that new horse."

"Where is he?" said Robbie, speaking fast. "Is he all right?"

"Of course," Father said. "I took him in before the storm struck. But as Mother was saying, we were glad you had Wally. He has horse sense. We didn't worry greatly."

"Speak for yourself, John," Mother said.

All of them were talking in such an ordinary way. Sarah couldn't believe it.

"Well, Sarah! What's the matter with you?" Here—" Father took charge of Blackie. "You'd better get indoors. You're chilled."

"But—but the wheat! All the lovely wheat! And the leaves on the trees! And the grass! Everything looks sick—it looks dead."

"She's worried about the car," said Robbie, trying to make a joke of it.

Father didn't laugh. "Into the house with you, Princess. And remember Who it was Who gave the wheat—and has the right to take it again, if this pleases Him."

The kitchen smelled of vanilla. On the cabinet was a pan

full of eggs and sugar and cream all sort of heaped together. Mother came in and took up the mixing spoon. "I'm making ice cream," she told Sarah.

Just then the screen door closed, and Father came in with his hail balls. The Scotts had no freezer. So Father brought a large tub from the woodshed. Mother poured the sweet vanilla mixture into a two-gallon tin syrup pail and pressed down the lid. Father put the pail in the tub and began packing hail balls and salt, in layers, around the pail—all the way to the rim. Then he began twirling the handle of the pail.

Sarah sat on the floor, leaning on the tub. She stared at the bobbing, churning hail balls. The salt was making them soupy, fast. But Father just added more balls and salt. Before long he opened the pail to stir the mixture. The stuff that clung to the edges of the pail was stiffening. He pushed it down and away, so the liquid part could flow in to take its place.

"It's coming," he said to Mother. "Well, Sarah, no chores to do today?"

Mother said quickly and rather quietly, "Do you think she should—today?" They looked at each other in a peculiar way.

"Why not?" said Father then. "She'll have to hear it sooner or later."

So they told her. The storm had damaged more than the wheat. It had killed all the goslings and many of the chicks. About 50 of them. Because the weather was so fine, they had been sunning themselves in the wire enclosure near the brooder house. There wasn't time to herd them all through the little door when the hail came. Goslings are especially stupid in matters like that. Chicks are smarter. The goslings simply piled into a corner of the enclosure. Those that weren't flattened by the hailstones were suffocated by the weight of other goslings on top of them.

Sarah felt sick. How *could* God? How could He allow things like this to happen? There were worse things still. Like wars and earthquakes and ships sinking at sea. And look at today. Such a perfect, perfect morning—and now—now —and Mr. Slocum, who usually made fun of God and the Bible—Mr. Slocum's fields were safe!

"Penny for your thoughts, Princess," said Father confidentially.

So she told him. She just plain spilled all her hurting thoughts out there beside the ice cream tub. "It isn't fair! It isn't fair!"

"Hush, Sarah." Father sounded almost stern. "But—we'll talk about this later. Away with you now."

Most of the hail balls outdoors were melting. The yard was a squishy flat of grass stalks, roots, ice, and mud. Outside the door of the brooder house stood the wheelbarrow. On it was a heap of chicks and goslings. Dead. But inside the chicks still shrieked at her, "Cheep, cheep, cheep!" Only, there wasn't the usual soft peelee-peelee sound coming from the goslings' corner.

It seemed to Sarah, as she filled the troughs and water jars, that she had never felt more sad and puzzled in her life. But when she stepped outside, Ginger and Bouncer came to meet her, and the wheelbarrow was gone.

Then there was Blackie to rub down and brush. They were becoming better friends every day. That helped now. Blackie's coat, silky and smooth, and her firm, well-shaped body and soft, nuzzling lips—all comforted Sarah today.

The new horse was back in the corral. When Sarah had finished her chores, she ran out to where Father and the boys, all three, sat on the rails, looking at the bay and discussing his fine points. And Robbie was proud—proud. He was going to call the horse *Bayard!*

"Sounds good to me," said Father. "OK, gang. Supper's waiting, I shouldn't wonder. Who's ready for a feed of ice cream?"

But at the table Father paused before he began to pray. *What'll he say today?* thought Sarah.

He began, "We thank You, Our heavenly Father, that *all* Your ways are right and just—" He thanked God for keeping Sarah and Robbie safe, and for a comfortable home, and that all of them were well, and well-fed. And that they all were Christians through Jesus' death and resurrection. And that they could trust their future to Him. He ended, "Bless this food. May it truly be a feast of praise."

A feast of praise— A feast of praise— The words sent a tingle through Sarah. All through supper they were there, like soft-toned bells in her mind.

Talk flowed around the table. Father said cheerfully that if the roots of the wheat hadn't been damaged, it would grow again. They'd wait a few days to see. If it grew, it was likely to be sturdier and yield more heads of wheat per plant, because that's the way the laws of nature—God's laws—worked. The wheat would be a week or two later than usual. But if God kept back the frosts, the grain could still do all right.

Keith told again how Aunt Jane made him promise to pick a good horse for Robbie—and not to say anything to anyone about it. "The Old Girl certainly enjoyed being on the scene this morning."

Sarah squished her spoon into the ice cream and took her first mouthful. *A feast of praise,* she thought.

After supper, while Mother and Sarah were at the corral, watching Robbie ride Bayard, their neighbor Slocum came driving up the lane, slithering from side to side. He was grinning as he waved to Father.

"Well, John!" he said, as soon as the engine was quiet. "Seems the Lord made a little mistake—a mite muddled, like."

And he laughed his high tee-hee-hee laugh. "Here's you and Him supposed to be on such friendly terms. He takes your grain and leaves mine. How do you account for that? S'pose He's gettin' a mite short-sighted, so He don't know who lives on what side of the fence? Got any texts to cover the situation?"

Sarah felt Mother stiffen. But Father looked even kinder than usual, though serious.

"Yes, I believe I have, Bill. Here's yours: 'Despisest thou the riches of His goodness and forebearance and longsuffering, not knowing that the goodness of God leadeth thee to repentance?'"

"Now, now John—"

"And here's mine: 'The Lord hath given, the Lord hath taken away, blessed be the name of the Lord." He gave Mother a sort of half-hug, but he looked Mr. Slocum straight in the eye.

Their neighbor shook his head in a puzzled way. He wasn't laughing anymore. In fact, he didn't make a single sound, but his engine roared suddenly.

"Poor man!" murmured Mother when the car went slipping and sliding down the driveway again.

"Never though the day would come when Slocum would be speechless," said Father. "Well, Princess—who's richer tonight, he or we?"

"We!"

Having God as your friend, that's the richest you can get, thought Sarah.

CHAPTER 5

SARAH TURNS DETECTIVE

THINGS TURNED OUT just the way Father hoped they would. Grass grew again. Many trees put out new yellowy-green leaves. And in a week or so the rolling fields were green again. The grain would be late, said Father. About 10 days late. But if the autumn frosts stayed away till September, there might even be a bumper crop! It all depended on the sunshine and the rains. And that was the same as saying it all depended on God.

And we can buy the car, thought Sarah, hugging the thought to herself. She seldom talked about it anymore.

One Saturday afternoon in late May, Sarah rode to Keith's ranch. He wasn't in the barn or house, so she left Blackie at the corral. She ran down a little ravine, crossed the creek on stepping stones, then climbed up the opposite hill. From there she could see his band of horses grazing. But no Keith.

Then she heard the chink of bridles, and Keith and Louise Thatcher came riding along the creek bank. Sarah grinned. She picked up a stone, intending to plop it into the water right in front of Masquerade.

But Keith was talking. "You're *sure*, Louise?" he said, sounding downhearted.

"It's the only thing I am sure about," said Louise. "Keith, I'm too young. Besides—"

"Besides what?"

"Besides, I've always dreamed of being a teacher. I always meant to go to Normal school a year to learn how to become a teacher, then have a year or two of teaching. If I don't, I think I'll always be sorry." She looked very pretty, pleading with Keith like this.

"And if you do? Say you have the two years? What then?"

"I can't promise anything. Not a thing, Keith. Could we— couldn't we just agree to be good friends?"

"*Friends!* Friendship wasn't what I had in mind, darling." He sounded as if he had a cold.

"I know, but—"

The horses stood, drinking from the creek. When they raised their heads, Sarah could hear water dripping from their muzzles, everything was so quiet. This conversation was private. Sarah shouldn't have been listening. But she never thought of covering her ears.

It wasn't really a secret that Keith thought Louise Thatcher awfully pretty and nice. All of Braeburn knew that. She *was* too. She had ripply auburn hair and a complexion like wild rose petals. And she walked tall and proud. She was smart too. In June she would write grade 12 exams. She would be the first Braeburn girl to go clear through high school!

Keith had hoped she'd say "yes," and they'd get married when she graduated. Everybody had thought it was just as good as settled. Every Sunday in church Sarah would wait for a special smile from Louise. *We're going to be sisters,* the smile seemed to say.

It was a remembering smile too. Because Sarah was with

Keith the day last winter when he saved Louise from an angry bull!

Afterward, Louise had thought Keith pretty wonderful, but now—

Keith was staring at the hillcrest or perhaps at the sky above it. "I have a dream," he said slowly. "It's worth waiting for—if necessary—worth being patient for. I promise, I'll not mention the subject again—for two years. Meanwhile you're free as the air."

"Thanks, Keith." They grasped hands and looked at each other for a long time. Then they rode slowly away. When Sarah got back to the corral, Louise was riding off in the distance. Keith didn't feel like visiting, so Sarah rode home. But he must have told Father about Louise that evening. And Father told Mother as they sat in the parlor when Sarah was supposed to be doing her fractions.

Usually Saturday night was singing time at the Scott home. Tonight Keith hadn't stayed for supper. And Robbie was riding Bayard once more before bedtime. And Stuart was studying hard for the final grade 12 exams. From the kitchen Sarah could hear Father's rocker creaking.

Mother said, "She might have told him earlier!"

And Father said, mildly, "Maybe he never gave her a chance before."

And Mother said, "Nonsense! Everybody knew what his hopes were. A girl can find ways to discourage unwelcome attentions if she really wants to."

"Well, she's young," said Father. "Inexperienced. And no doubt she was flattered by his attentions. But if he holds to his present resolve, this may be the making of him. Had you thought of that, Sheila? It may put some needed backbone into our charming son."

The rocking chair creaked again.

"Sarah," called Mother. "Bedtime for you. The bath water and tub are ready in the woodshed."

"Aren't we going to have any singing?"

"Not tonight."

"Oh, now, Mother," Father coaxed. "Just one song?"

So they sang his favorite, "Have Thine Own Way, Lord." At the end, the organ gave a long, sad sigh.

Sarah blurted out, "Do families always hurt? I mean, if something sad happens to one person, do the others always hurt?"

Father rubbed the top of her head the way he did when he was especially fond of her. "Always," he said. "Always. If they *love* each other. It's part of loving."

Mother said, softly, "Think how the heart of God must have been wrung when Jesus hung on the cross for us. Or when His beloved Son cried out, 'My God, My God, why hast Thou forsaken Me?'"

And Father added, "And think of how Christ's heart was broken for the sin and sorrow of the world—He who loved us so much. Off with you now, Princess."

She went to bed, but not to sleep. Not right away. At first she thought about Keith and Louise. But the thoughts that whirled in her mind were not all sad, solemn ones. She had found out the Chernishenko secret! She didn't know *all* of it, but she had a pretty good notion of some of it.

Today, after returning from Keith's place, she raced barefoot down the hill to round up the cows. However, they had come home from the pasture on their own, because milking time had been delayed. They lay near the old strawpile, chewing their cuds.

The pile looked like a huge brown toadstool. As high as the cows could reach, they had eaten away the straw so that the lower part looked like the stem of a toadstool. Holes in the strawpile opened into zigzag tunnels that ran all the way through to the other side.

In winter the calves and yearling were never taken indoors. When the fiercest blizzards blew, they were snug in the tunnels. The straw was both their food and shelter. But in summer! In summer the tunnels made a dandy hide-and-seek place on Sunday afternoons when the Gerricks or some other families came to visit.

As Sarah came running toward the strawpile, she saw Robbie in one of the tunnel openings. She thought it was Robbie. Then she heard Bouncer barking in the meadow beyond the corral—and there was Robbie, giving Bayard a good workout. She swung round again. The boy, whoever he was, had backed farther into the tunnel. He was watching Robbie.

Sarah pretended not to see him. She nudged the cows with her bare heel, and one by one they groaned and got to their feet. Then, as always, Brindle led them swaying, up the hill to the barn for milking.

Robbie came to do his share of the milking while Sarah tended to the chicks and gathered the eggs. Afterward—when it was almost dark—she saw Robbie riding slowly across the meadow toward Aunt Jane's place. Someone about his size was walking on the far side of the horse.

Sarah lay in bed thinking about it. She remembered the day Aunt Jane "saw" Robbie in the barn—when he wasn't there at all! And how *Mrs.* Chernishenko acted when Sarah looked into the wagonload of secondhand furniture. And when Sarah wanted to say thank-you for the egg, Mrs. Chernishenko hadn't wanted Sarah to see inside her house! They were hiding something—or someone. This boy, maybe? But *why?*

Sarah was still tingling with curiosity when she awoke the

next morning. Robbie would be able to tell them everything. Who the boy was—where he came from—why he was a secret. Everything.

But—he didn't. He did his chores as usual. He ate his breakfast and went to church. As usual. He didn't say a single word about the stranger. Now, knowing there's a secret makes you tingle with excitement—for a while. But if the *while* goes on and on, it becomes a bother. You can't concentrate on anything else.

Then who should come to dinner with them but Aunt Jane! Mother hadn't even invited her. She had invited the Slocums and the Heathes. They were neighbors who almost never went to church, so they usually came to visit on weekdays. But today Mother had invited them especially, and this morning the Slocums had even been to church.

The whole tableful of people were grown-ups except Robbie and Sarah. So most of the talk was grown-up talk. Like, "When I homesteaded here in 1906—" Or, "When my pa and ma came west in 1880—" And the ladies talked about their gardens. Mrs. Slocum's garden hardly had any hail at all. It was doing very well. Everybody knew she would share her vegetables and flowers with all Braeburn. She was like that. She was a noisy lady, with a booming kind of voice, but everybody said her heart was in the right place.

Take the time Aunt Jane was in the hospital with a broken hip last fall. It had happened at the busiest time of all the year—threshing time. Because of that, Mother had to feed 40 men on one day. Two threshing machines had come the same day—one to Aunt Jane's place, one to the Scott place. Mother said afterwards that she wouldn't have known what to do if it hadn't been for Mabel Slocum.

Mrs. Slocum took Sarah to town with her and bought a mountain of groceries. Then she stopped at all the farms along the way and asked the ladies to help. They did too. Some baked cakes and pies and things. Some came to help serve the food. Everybody was kind. But it was all on account of Mabel Slocum. She was a good organizer.

And there was the time, later in the fall, when Father and Mother had gone with Aunt Jane to Ontario where she would stay with her brother. Mrs. Slocum did the washing and house-cleaning and baking for Sarah and Robbie and Stuart, so they could go to school.

Whenever Sarah saw Mrs. Slocum, she remembered all the helping times. But Mrs. Slocum wasn't a Christian. Well, her husband wasn't either. And he was a dreadful tease. Often his teasing was like needles pricking into you. He enjoyed laughing then—but nobody else did, much. And today he was pricking Aunt Jane. And she was getting pink and pinker. Finally Mrs. Slocum said, sort of rumbling, "OK, now. You just simmer down, Dad."

And he simmered down. But he winked at Sarah as he helped himself to more roast ham, mashed potatoes, and gravy.

Then Father seemed to think it was his turn to ask questions of Aunt Jane. "How have the Chernishenkos been lately?"

Well, *that* wasn't a very happy subject either. "Mind you, John," said Aunt Jane. "I have no complaint about their work. Both of them work hard. But something is wrong somewhere, some secret sorrow or worry. I can't explain it. But it's hanging over them constantly—and the situation seems to be getting worse."

Sarah's heart thumped. She slid a look at Robbie beside her. He went on drinking water, not looking at anyone.

"Sarah? Sarah, dear," said Mother. "Remove the plates, please."

Dessert was saskatoon berry pie, Sarah's favorite. So, for a while, she almost forgot the mystery. But when dinner was over and she was excused from drying dishes because there were so many ladies to do it, she raced to join Robbie at the corral.

He wasn't riding today. This was Sunday, so Robbie was wearing his second-best suit. He was sitting on the topmost pole and talking to his horse, coaxing him to come closer, just by the sound of his voice. Head up, ears alert, Bayard came, a few steps at a time. Then he reached out a slender neck to snuffle at Robbie.

Breathless from her run, Sarah slammed against the fence. Bayard's head came up with a jerk and a snort, and he circled away at a gallop.

"Aw, why'd you go and spoil it?" said Robbie. "Here, Bayard, boy. Come here."

"Forget about your old horse for a minute," Sarah said. "Who's the boy over at Chernishenkos'? That's what I want to know."

"What are you talking about?" said Robbie, not looking at her.

"You know."

Robbie kicked his heels, whistled through his teeth, and frowned at the treetops along the creek.

"Who is he? I saw him, so it's no good saying there isn't anybody. Come on. Tell."

"Where? When?" said Robbie.

"Yesterday. When you were riding Bayard, and I was hurrying up the lazy cows. He was in the strawpile tunnel. And afterwards I saw you walking Bayard across the meadow, and someone was walking beside you. I could see his legs. So there!"

Robbie still drummed his heels and whistled that hissing whistle.

"Tell!" urged Sarah impatiently.

"Can't."

"Why not? Did you promise the Chernishenkos you wouldn't?"

Robbie whistled away.

"I'll go in and tell Aunt Jane that there's a stupid secret—and that you know about it."

"Go ahead," said Robbie. "See if I care."

Sarah marched away. But she didn't go into the house. She liked ferreting out secrets for herself. That was much more fun than getting grown-ups to help. So her first stop was at her secret thinking place under the crab apple tree.

Almost immediately she felt a cold nose poking at her—and there was Bouncer, with Ginger not far behind. Bouncer was big and woolly now, and more bouncy than ever. He never whimpered at night, but Ginger still seemed to feel responsible for him. Since Bayard's arrival, Robbie hadn't spent as much time with the pup as he had before, so Bouncer had taken to following Sarah.

With one furry friend sitting on her tummy, licking her chin, and another purring in her ears, Sarah thought of all the bits and pieces that she knew or thought she knew about the Chernishenko mystery. She was trying to get up enough courage to go over to the Chernishenkos', now that Aunt Jane was safely out of the way. She decided nobody must see her go, so she dumped Bouncer and Ginger, and crawled out of her hiding place.

She raced to the end of the path, crawled through a caragana hedge, under bushy maple trees, and rolled under the barbed wire fence into the meadow.

Bouncer came trotting after her—and Ginger after Bouncer—but at the creek the puppy stopped. He didn't like the looks of the stepping stones.

"OK. Stay there," called Sarah. She was in too big a hurry to help an unhappy puppy over the creek.

Aunt Jane's yard was the neatest farmyard ever. That showed what good workers the Chernishenkos were. The hens with their half-grown chicks were all neatly penned up in a high, wire enclosure. That was new. Mr. Chernishenko had built it for Aunt Jane.

But Sarah had one thing on her mind. Her heart was thumping. She thought of the last time she went to see Mrs. Chernishenko. The boy must have been indoors then, and the lady hadn't wanted Sarah to peek in.

Today there was no chance to hide him. Sarah walked quietly down the garden path and suddenly appeared in the gap in the caragana hedge. The Chernishenkos were sitting outdoors. With them was the boy.

"Hello," said Sarah politely. "May I come to visit?"

Almost immediately she was sorry she had come. The boy smiled and looked friendly. But Mrs. Chernishenko was frightened, then angry. She and her husband shouted at each other, talking very fast in a strange language. Mr. Cherni-shenko seemed to be trying to calm her down, but she was talking and crying. It was a mix-up.

Then the lady turned on Sarah. "Your brodder. He say he no tal. Iss not goot! Not goot!"

"Please, Mrs. Chernishenko," begged Sarah. "Robbie *didn't* tell. He didn't break his promise." She swung round to face the boy. "You tell them. Tell them where I saw you."

But that minute a great racket broke out in the yard. Chickens cackling and squawking. A dog barking. Bouncer! He must have followed her after all. And now he'd got into mischief.

Sarah raced down the garden path. She could hear the Chernishenkos pounding along behind her. There was a little door in the new chicken pen. It was low down for chickens to go in and out. It had been closed before. Bouncer must have nosed it open accidentally, because he and Ginger were inside. He sat up against the fence, barking. And all the mother hens took turns fluttering in and out, trying to peck at him. Ginger sat there, blinking at them, and whenever a hen got too close to Bouncer, Ginger would swat at her with her paw. Smack! She sent another squawking hen fluttering backward.

It looked so funny. A moment ago Sarah had felt awful. Now she began laughing and couldn't stop. The Chernishenkos began laughing too. They whooped together, slapping their sides, and bending down to catch their breath. They made more noise than the hens.

"Well, well, well!" said a voice. And there stood Aunt Jane!

That was a strange moment. Everyone was silent. Even the hens! Only Bouncer still gave a few half-hearted woofs. Mrs. Chernishenko looked as though she might burst out crying again.

But Aunt Jane said briskly, "How about taking the pup out of the cage, Sarah. Then come to the house, all of you. I think it's high time we had a talk to clear the air."

"Yes, Missis," said Mrs. Chernishenko meekly.

Sarah trembled as she pulled Bouncer out. (He didn't want to come, the rascal! He'd been having a perfectly lovely time! But Ginger seemed glad not to have to defend him against the fierce hens anymore.) Suddenly Sarah had the shakes from all the excitement. She was sure she'd hear about the mystery now. And she was right.

The boy's name, it seemed, was Evahn Evahnovitch— That's the way it sounded. His parents died on the ship, coming to Canada from Russia. When he landed in Montreal, the Canadian government didn't know what to do with him. But the

Chernishenkos had come on the same ship. Their two children had died in the Ukraine, so they said they would take him.

"That was a fine thing," said Aunt Jane. Everyone was seated on her lawn, sipping lemonade and nibbling cookies Mrs. Chernishenko had made. "But why did you try to *hide* the boy?"

"And do you know, Father," said Sarah later, when she was pouring out the whole story at home. "Do you know? The Chernishenkos said it was on account of *you.* They said you told them they'd better have no children if they wanted to work for Aunt Jane."

"Now, wait a minute!" Father exclaimed.

"Go on, Sarah," Mother encouraged, with a tiny smile at Father. "John, you can state your defense later."

"Well," continued Sarah, "Mr. Chernishenko needed the job. And Mrs. Chernishenko liked the chance to have her own little house to herself again. It was her idea to hide Evahn O-Witch— I *think* that's his name. But he got fed up with hiding all the time."

"Well, I should think *so!*" said Father. "No, Sheila, now it's my turn," he said firmly to Mother. "When I interviewed them for the job, I asked if they had children, and they said no. And I said that perhaps it was just as well. Jane Bolton had been ill, and having youngsters around might be too much for her. That's all I said."

Just then Robbie came into the kitchen, and Father turned to him. "Son, what do you know about the boy over at Chernishenkos?"

Robbie's face reddened, but Sarah said quickly, "It's no secret anymore. It's all right. Aunt Jane knows all about it."

Robbie expelled a long sigh. "Ah, about time! It was a dumb secret anyway. But they were so scared, I had to promise. And I have to keep a promise, don't I?"

Robbie called the boy Ivan. Ivan Ivanson. That's what his name meant, he said. "And don't you ever go and call him O'Witch in school, Sarah Scott!" he warned.

School! But of course. Ivan would go to Braeburn now, since he had been discovered. He was only 13.

The past two months he had come out of hiding after dark and helped in the barn. That was where Robbie met him one evening.

One thing that made Sarah laugh now was the realization that Ivan had been hidden in the wagon under the chairs and the mattress that first day. When she hopped up to poke around among the secondhand furniture, Mrs. Chernishenko had been afraid she'd find Ivan.

"The moral," said Father, "is, don't go poking into other people's affairs." But he was smiling. Sarah had gone poking today, and it had turned out for the best. "But don't you make a habit of it, young lady."

"The moral," said Sarah, pointing at Robbie, "is, don't make stupid promises."

"The moral," said Mother, laughing as she pointed at Father, "is, be sure you make yourself clearly understood when you are hiring help for somebody else."

It was a silly game they were all playing. But having silly jokes together is a part of being a happy family.

CHAPTER 6

NEW BOY AT BRAEBURN

SARAH SCOTT came from the barn carrying two pails half full of milk. In the yard, Robbie and Ivan Chernishenko were playing ball. That's the way it was at the Scotts' these days. That's the way it would be until the end of June.

On June 1st Father had made one of his announcements at breakfast. Except on Sundays, from now on until Stuart and Robbie's final exams were over, they would be excused from doing chores. They had to study. Keith had offered to come over from his ranch every night and morning to help.

"That means, Sarah," said Mother, "that you and I will need to divide Robbie's work between us. You will keep the wood-box filled."

"On top of everything else?" exclaimed Sarah. "Feeding the chicks and gathering the eggs—and everything?"

"On top of everything else," said Mother.

"You'll also milk Brindle," decided Father.

Sarah made a face at Robbie who was grinning at her.

"No grumpiness, now, Princess," Father had said, tapping her head as he rose to leave the table. "Remember, the boys lost a lot of studying time while helping with the spring work. Be glad you're not a boy."

Spring work. That meant plowing and harrowing and seeding. Sarah remembered the days when Robbie stayed home from school to walk all day after the harrow, pulled by four horses. He had walked about 30 miles a day, over soft-plowed land. He'd been so tired at night, he could hardly eat his supper. So—maybe it was fair that he got excused now. But Sarah still didn't like it.

Of course, Robbie's playing ball was mostly for Ivan's sake. The new boy was attending Braeburn school now, a great big boy of 13, reading baby stories in grade one books. As a ball player he had belonged in the first grade too. He couldn't throw a ball properly, and he couldn't bat worth a cent.

He could run though. But that was another of Sarah's troubles. Robbie insisted on going to school with Ivan. Each morning now, if Ivan wasn't ready, Robbie waited for him at Aunt Jane's driveway. At first Sarah waited with him. But Ivan didn't have a horse. He would come running, and boy and horses would go trotting along. Ivan, barefoot like the others at Braeburn school, ran on the grass beside the road.

Ivan had a fast springy trot for a boy, but pokey for a horse. Blackie didn't like being held back and she didn't like waiting. Neither did Sarah. So now that she had Robbie's chores to do, she usually left home later—and went another way to school.

In school Ivan would probably have had a rough time if it hadn't been for Robbie. He was the big boy in Braeburn now. He didn't boss anybody much. He was a good student, a good ball player, and he stuck up for all the small children. And he wasn't ashamed to chum with an overgrown grade oner!

So Ivan had a pretty easy time, in a way. And Robbie was trying to make it easier. That was why Ivan came over every evening to practice throwing and batting a softball. Robbie was proud and pleased at how fast he was catching on.

He was a Chernishenko now. Aunt Jane Bolton had hired a lawyer for the Chernishenkos, and they were going to adopt him as soon as the papers could be straightened out. Chernishenko still was a hard name, but it certainly sounded better than that Ivanovitch name. "That O'Witch name," Sarah called it at home one day. But Robbie turned on her, and for once he looked really fierce. "If I ever catch you calling Ivan that in school, I'll—I'll—"

"You'll what?"

"I'll give you a good shaking."

"O'Witch. O'Witch," Sarah teased. Of course, she'd never dream of saying it in school. She could just imagine what some of the pupils would do with a chance like that to tease a newcomer.

They couldn't do a thing as long as Robbie was around, of course. But when exam time came, he'd be going to Blakely every day to write them. Then there'd be no Robbie around to stick up for Ivan.

Apart from the extra chores, June was Sarah's favorite month. Nights were cool but mornings were crisp and sunny. Days were long and full of things to do. Susan was cramming hard for finals at school. She reviewed all the facts and dates over and over. But Sarah remembered history stories and loved to tell them on paper. She liked writing compositions. She'd pass, she guessed. It was nice not to have to worry. You could enjoy the lovely things about June.

In the middle of June, roses came out. Oh, millions of them, all along the fence rows. And meadowlarks sang from fence and telephone posts. In one particular bush along the road Sarah had seen a pair of orioles, black and orangy red, flashing back and forth. As she rode to and from school, she stopped to try to find their nest. It was too cleverly hidden. Besides, Blackie was restless if she snubbed her to a post too long. But she could hear the oriole call: "Pewter! Pewter!"

Every year, a couple of wrens nested in an old Rawleigh's Black Pepper box that Father had nailed to a poplar tree one spring. They had come again. Their trill kept Sarah cheerful while she milked old Brindle. She would hear the crack of the bat outside, when Ivan hit the ball.

"Good going!" she heard Robbie shout. "Won't we wow the Braeburn bunch one of these days!"

It was sort of a joke. At school each day Robbie, who was the school pitcher, still threw careful baby balls at Ivan, and the new boy gave baby bunts. Then he'd race away. Because he could run, he'd get almost halfway round the diamond before he was stopped. Nobody guessed it was all sham now. He was getting to be a *good* player. Robbie was getting him ready for the school picnic at the end of the school year. People came for miles around for that. The school team always played the outsiders.

This evening, just as Sarah was crossing the yard with her two half pails of milk, Father came home from the field. His face and hands were black with dust, so that his teeth looked very white when he talked or smiled. Robbie and Ivan ran to lift the harness off the backs of the six horses. They snorted and shook their withers and lay down right where they were. Before you knew it, 24 hooves were waving and swaying in the air. Sarah ran to get out of their way.

Also she could hear the cream separator humming. That meant that Mother might be waiting for Brindle's milk. After the separating, Sarah would have to help Robbie feed the calves. That was one chore he still had every evening. The baby bulls were too ornery for Sarah to manage alone.

When Father came in for supper, Mother sent Sarah running to meet him at the door with soft clean cloths. He wiped his face and hands with them, then dusted his shoulders and arms. He even asked Sarah to sweep across his back with the broom before he would step inside.

This was the last Friday evening before exams began. Monday, Robbie would ride to town, to high school, for the first time. Next year, if he wanted to, he'd be going every day. Most farm boys didn't. But Father believed in education for boys. Keith would have finished high school if he hadn't run away in the middle of it. Stuart was going to finish this spring.

They had hash for supper—with pickles, bread and butter, skimmed milk, and crabapple sauce for dessert. And the family talk was sort of hashy too—a bit of this and a bit of that. Two of Keith's mares had had foals this week. Mother got a letter from Kathleen in California. (She and Herbie had hoped to come home for a month or so this summer, but Herbie would have to stay on the job to earn money for next year's studies.) At first, last fall, Sarah had felt as if she couldn't bear to have Kathleen so far away. Now it seemed unreal that she had ever been at home.

"I had so hoped they would come," said Mother with a sigh as she folded the letter.

"What about you, Stuart?" said Father suddenly. "Have you decided yet what to do with your future?"

"Is it to be normal training?" said Mother hopefully. That meant, "Do you plan to become a teacher?"

Mother used to teach. Sometimes she had talked about Stuart becoming a teacher—teaching at Braeburn and boarding at home. He'd be Sarah's teacher then, which would be strange but very nice.

"I'm—not—sure," said Stuart, and he looked as if he meant to drop the subject. But then he added, "I have a feeling God wants me to go to Bible school."

They all stared at him in astonishment. And Mother exclaimed, "Not to California! Not you too!"

Stuart smiled. "It's not the end of the world," he said. "But—Herbie's school is expensive—at least for us Scotts. There's a school in Alberta. Brother Hammond told me about it. Foothills Bible Institute. It's good, he says, and not expensive—and it emphasizes missions."

Mother gave him an odd look, but all she said was, "Stack the dishes, Sarah."

Afterwards, Sarah followed Stuart to the door of his room. "Are you—are you going to be a preacher like Herbie?" she whispered.

He smiled. "A missionary, I think."

A *missionary*. Then—then maybe he'd be going farther than Kathleen!

"Don't look so shocked, Sis," said Stuart gently. "When you love God, you want to obey Him. And I believe He is calling me to foreign service."

The ache in Sarah's heart kept her awake for a long time that night.

Stuart was special! Ever since last summer when Braeburn had a revival, Stuart was different. He had been nice before, but he was extra special now. When Sarah was in trouble, Stuart was the one who usually asked the right questions and gave the right answers.

Monday morning early he and Robbie were ready to ride to Blakely. Examinations began at 8:30. Robbie looked calm, sitting there on Bayard, but Sarah knew he wasn't. He'd only had half a helping of porridge and no pancakes at all! Robbie usually ate a good breakfast and *loved* pancakes.

"Do you have your fountain pen—your ink and foolscap?" called Father, who was hitching his six-horse team in the yard. "Make a good job of your exams."

The boys waved, and away they rode. This was an important day.

Sarah felt strange—a little cross, a little sad, a little empty. A sort of no-sorts-at-all feeling. And she had to help Mother feed the calves before she could start for school.

That morning Ivan looked lost in school without Robbie. Chuckie Gerrick was writing grade eight exams too. So were Grace Millar and Violetta Siddons. All the big pupils were away this week. Perhaps that was why there was such a spirit of mischief in school. But Sarah still never knew what made her tell the middle-sized girls about the O'Witch part of Ivan's name.

It was enough. More than enough. At recess and at noon, instead of playing softball or Prisoner's Base, Braeburn pupils ganged up on the new boy to tease him. He didn't fight back or get angry. But once he turned and looked at Sarah. And *that* was enough.

Once, on a First-of-July family picnic, Sarah had found a squirrel with its feet caught in a trap. It had looked at her, eyes full of pain and fear and reproach. Ivan's eyes reminded her of that squirrel's. She felt the meanest she had ever felt in all her life. And the feeling stayed with her wherever she went.

A couple of days later, she heard Father say, "What's made our girl so quiet these days?"

And Mother said, "So you noticed it too? I do hope she isn't coming down with something."

Stuart, when he wasn't away, was too busy studying to notice. Robbie still played ball with Ivan every evening, but the new boy must have kept quiet about the way he was being treated in school each day now. Sarah never looked at him if she could help it. She felt too guilty. She would have caught it if Robbie had known. He didn't get angry quickly.

But when someone was cruel to someone, watch out!

That's the way things went until Thursday. Exams at Braeburn were over. Sarah had passed. Her marks might have been better if she hadn't had this trouble on her mind all the time. The thought that troubled her most of all was that she was a *Christian.*

Last summer she had received the Lord Jesus as her Saviour. She had asked Him to cleanse her and to come into her life to stay. And He had. She knew He had. But a Christian was supposed to *behave* like one. Every day she asked Jesus to forgive her—but it didn't make her feel any better. How could that be?

Susan Gerrick, Sarah's special friend, never joined in the teasing. Never. She must have guessed how Sarah felt, though they never talked about it. At noon they would sit together on the grass, eating their lunches and talking. They talked about the tests. Susan did better, as usual, in writing down the *facts.* But Sarah did better in using her imagination. They talked about how strange it would seem to have a new teacher next September. Mrs. Millar wasn't coming back. But they never mentioned Ivan and the Witch thing.

Just now the grade sevens and some of the sixes were at it again. Ivan was backed against a fence post. They stood around in a half circle, razzing and razzing him. No one noticed when a car stopped close by. The driver was Grant Millar, the nature lover man. In a minute he was out of the car and over the fence. He had long legs. He took hold of the shirt collars of two of Ivan's chief tormentors and pulled them away from the boy.

"What's this? Can't you find anything better to do with your time than to torment somebody? I'm ashamed of you!"

Teacher had just stepped outdoors to ring the bell. She heard what he said.

"What's wrong, Grant?" she called anxiously.

"As shameful a bit of boy-baiting as ever I've seen," he said. "But I'll leave you to deal with it."

And then he drove on and school was called.

Tomorrow afternoon was the school picnic. In the morning, they'd have a rehearsal of the school program. And Mrs. Millar would make her final speech to the boys and girls, and hand out the report cards and promotion certificates. After that they'd all leave for the picnic ground in Thatcher's pasture. So today was the final regular school day. And now everything was spoiled.

And it's your fault, Sarah Scott, said a voice deep inside her.

Teacher looked grave and anxious. She said maybe she had been too busy with their papers. She should have known what was going on in the school yard. Would someone please tell her what had happened?

Braeburn was quiet. No one moved. No one said a thing. The clock ticked loudly. Sarah's heart pounded—slowly and heavily. Through the open window came a breeze and the bubbling song of a meadowlark. Braeburn sat frozen.

"Can someone tell me what's wrong?" begged Teacher. Suddenly Sarah knew she must do the talking. She raised her hand.

"Yes, Sarah?" Teacher smiled encouragingly.

"I—it's—I guess it's my fault, really," she said. And she told how she had started the teasing by telling Ivan's real name, but twisting it a little.

Sarah was ashamed to look up. Teacher's voice sounded grave now.

"Thank you, Sarah. Thnak you for your honesty. But I'm sorry it was necessary."

Oh, so was Sarah! Now, whenever Mrs. Millar thought

about Sarah Scott, most likely she would think about what a sneaking thing she did to Ivan.

Teacher added, "Don't let me hear another whisper about this from any of you. Or I'll take appropriate steps."

That sounded fierce. Teacher was fair, but she was strict too. So when recess came no one knew how to act. Sarah had an idea, a shiny idea! Everyone, practically, was gathered on the softball diamond. She called to Bertie Gerrick, "Send a ball, a real sizzler, to Ivan."

Susan looked reproachfully at Sarah. She didn't know what Sarah knew! The other Braeburners liked the idea fine.

"Yeah, you do that, Bertie. Here's your bat, Ivan." They were very polite and helpful. They thought they were going to have more fun out of him. He'd swish the bat through empty air, maybe, or make a baby bunt. But Ivan gave Sarah a half smile as he gripped the bat. Then he turned to face Bertie.

There came the ball. Ivan's bat connected. Up and away went the ball. And there went Ivan, flying around the bases. Of course, it couldn't count as a homer. None of the fielders and basemen were in place. But they were impressed. They tried him again and again. He could really knock the ball. And no one could run the way Ivan could.

"Yay, Ivan!" they cheered. "Boy, we'll have you on the school team tomorrow. We'll clobber them outsiders!"

School was over early. All they did after recess was practice one dialogue for tomorrow and the school songs. Then, for the last time, they stood to sing, "Now the day is over; night is drawing nigh—"

"Sarah Scott, may I see you for a minute?" said Teacher. Then, "Class, dismissed."

Sarah's heart was beating uncomfortably. Susan gave her a frightened look. Some of the others grinned as they clattered out and left her alone with the noisy clock—and Teacher. Their looks said, "Now you'll catch it. I wouldn't want to be in your shoes."

Sarah wasn't wearing any, but she slid her bare feet restlessly over the floor, waiting, waiting—

"Come here, dear," said Teacher, just when it seemed as if Sarah couldn't stand it a moment longer. "No need to be frightened," she added, smiling. "I wanted to ask you a question or two. Why did you do it? Why did you—"

"I didn't mean to." The words tumbled out of Sarah's mouth. "I don't know why I told about the O'Witch thing. I never, never meant to."

"That's not what I meant," said Teacher. "What made you take the blame on yourself? What made you speak up?" She was looking down now, making tiny pencil marks on the paper before her.

"I—I didn't want to," said Sarah honestly. "I was scared to. But—in a way—I was more scared not to."

"Why was that?" And this time Teacher looked up earnestly.

"Well, because I love Jesus. And I knew it was a naughty thing I did. He was sorry. I could feel it. And I was sorry too. Awfully sorry. But I *had* to tell—don't you see? I had to *show* I was sorry."

Tears were dripping from Sarah's chin onto Teacher's desk. Teacher shook out a lovely clean hanky, all perfumey, and handed it to Sarah so she could mop her face.

"I—see," she said kindly. "I'm very glad I've learned to know a staunch little Christian like you, Sarah."

Next morning was report card time. And practice time. And Teacher's last-speech time. And last rehearsal time. Then came a quick lunch, and everyone hurried over to the picnic place.

The Union Jack flapping above the tops of the poplar bush showed everyone for miles around where the Braeburn picnic was to be. And they came. They came in cars mostly. But some came in lumbering wagons and buggies or on horseback. And Ivan was the star of the picnic. Really. Teacher called on him for a speech. This was an item on the program that no one else had known about. They'd had all the funny dialogues and recitations and songs—all the stuff they'd practiced for weeks. No one had heard anything about the speech.

"Ladees and Gantlemans," began Ivan. "My name, it was Evahn Evahnovitch. Now iss Ivan Chernishenko. I will tell you how it comes.

"I live in Roshia. I am born in Roshia. Then when I am chust four years, comes the Revolution. Many, many people die. From the Bolchewicks, and from the starvation. My fodder, he almost die from the Bolchewicks, but he comes free again. He saw we must go to a new gountry. (He meant *country*.) We try, and we try. Always it is no, and no. We cannot go. Then comes the day when we can go on the ship."

Sarah sat motionless, staring at Ivan. All the Braeburn pupils were listening as hard as ever they could. They forgot all about his strange way of talking. He told of how his parents both died at sea, and how the Chernishenkos took pity on him, and tried to hide him!

"Iss because we not know how kind iss this new gountry. We are afraid, all the time afraid. Like in old gountry. Now I have again a fodder and modder. I have again a home. I go to school. I learn many things. I learn to play ball! You will see once how I learn to play ball!"

Here all the Braeburn pupils laughed and clapped.

"So now. Iss all I want to say. I am happy for new fodder and modder, new home, new gountry. Iss everything new. And goot. So now maybe iss time I sit down."

And he did. And now everybody clapped for Ivan and his speech. Father, who was asked to make a few remarks, said it was one of the finest, most inspiring speeches he had ever heard!

Later, on the ball field, Robbie and Ivan demonstrated their teamwork. The new boy's batting was good. But his running was even better. Well, when you practice running by racing a horse every day, you *have* to be good.

He wasn't going to be a new boy for very long.

CHAPTER 7

A SURPRISE FOR SARAH

SARAH DIDN'T actually *mind* summer holidays. But after a week or so, they became rather everydayish. Morning, noon, and evening she had to dry dishes. In between there was the garden to weed—and the job never got *done*. You pulled the pesky weeds one week—and next week they were back, growing like sixty. The *same ones,* it seemed.

Some in-between-days weren't quite so busy. Then Sarah might ride Blackie around the pasture for an hour, trying to teach her some tricks. Or she'd take a favorite book and, with Bouncer and Ginger at her heels, she'd go down to the creek. She and Bouncer would tumble in and out of the water for a while, having fun, while Ginger sat on the bank, watching and worrying.

Then Bouncer and Ginger would go off to chase butterflies, beetles, and dragonflies. And Sarah would curl up against the knobby roots of a poplar, and read, and dream— Always, she dreamt that she was someone else, living someplace else, doing interesting, exciting things.

This morning Sarah expected to have an everydayish day.

Last night Mother had said cheerfully, "Well, Sarah, tomorrow it's the garden patch for you and me again."

Sarah groaned as she bit into a sugar cooky.

"Might as well put a cheerful face and happy heart into the job. It has to be done, and that's that." Then Mother added, "Sarah, Sarah, how *brown* you're getting. Your hair is bleaching sadly. We'll have to put a sunbonnet on you."

"Oh, *no!*" wailed Sarah. Wearing a sunbonnet was the *worst* thing on a hot day.

"I don't have to, do I, Father?"

"Your mother will have to decide that," was all he said. But Sarah knew he didn't care for sunbonnets on girls any more than she did. He didn't *mind* a suntanned girl, even it it wasn't fashionable. So—maybe—Mother would forget about the sunbonnet nonsense.

With a cheerful face and a happy heart, thought Sarah, the moment she awoke this morning. At first she thought, *Ho-hum,* and made a little face. Then she remembered—she belonged to the Lord Jesus, and He belonged to her. And she really did want to please Him. He could help her be pleasant, if she asked Him. So she did.

Afterward, she skimmed down the stairs to see what Mother had fixed for breakfast. The table was untidy because Father and the boys had eaten long ago and gone to the field. The men had porridge for breakfast, and French toast with pin-cherry jelly or Roger's Golden Syrup.

A few slices of stale bread were waiting for her, and some of the egg and milk mixture. Mother was at the telephone, so Sarah moved the frying pan to the front of the stove, where it was hottest, and dipped a slice of bread in the egg-mix. Both sides. When the fat was hot she dropped the slice in. It sizzled, and the smell made Sarah's mouth water.

Mother was saying, "Well, how nice for you, Jane. Well,

Sarah and I were planning to weed the garden— Yes? After all, weeds don't run away— Of course— Of course—" And she laughed. "Yes, Sarah's down. Good-bye for now."

Sarah perked up her ears hopefully. *Weeds don't run away.* That sounded as if . . . ?

"Are you and Aunt Jane going some place?"

"Good morning, Sarah. We might—and we might not—go to Paxton. But the point is, you won't be required to weed the garden." She sounded enormously pleased about something. Sarah was about to ask more questions when Mother said, "Sarah! Your toast!"

It was beginning to burn. Sarah lifted it out of the pan. She didn't mind a bit of charcoal.

She ate that slice and fried another. She was busy trying to decide which of her favorite books would be right for the poplar grove down at the creek this morning. It was a warm, reading kind of morning. Sarah was glad clear through that she needn't chop weeds.

After the breakfast dishes were done, she raced outdoors, hugging a tattered copy of *Little Women* to her. Her sister Kathleen got the book for her 12th birthday, 10 years ago. Sarah's gingham dress was cool and light. Her bare feet padded on the rough grainy concrete of the walk, and out through the garden gate.

As usual Bouncer came galloping after her, yelping and mumbling happily and anxiously. *Don't leave me. Wait for me.* And of course, Ginger wasn't far behind. The water in the creek winked at Sarah. The poplar leaves clapped for her. And four storybook girls waited for her to get settled down on her favorite spot. Sarah turned to one of her favorite chapters that told of a long-ago picnic.

The sudden snapping of a twig made her head come up with a jerk. There stood Susan Gerrick! Sarah's eyes almost popped. Susan was smiling and looking excited, and terribly, terribly pleased. Sarah couldn't believe her eyes. Susan almost never got to go visiting on weekdays. She had many more chores at home than Sarah did, even if she was a few months younger.

"It's—it's like another make-believe," said Sarah, hugging her friend.

"I'm not the biggest surprise," said Susan. "Someone else is here. Look there, up the hill."

And, coming carefully down the hill, was a girl about their own age. She was slender and had blond curls. And she was walking on her own two feet—Linda Bolton! Sarah's very special friend from Ottawa, Aunt Jane's niece. A year ago she couldn't walk a step, because she was so badly crippled from polio. *Linda.*

Sarah ran to meet her, with chubby Susan pounding after. *Linda, Linda, Linda.* The name was like a song in Sarah's throat, but she couldn't make a sound. They met in a three-way hug, squealing and laughing and breathless.

Beyond, near the corral, stood Aunt Jane Bolton and Mother. Now Sarah knew why her mother had postponed the weeding.

But the surprises were not over. Mrs. Slocum, the Scott's neighbor, came driving into the yard in her Model T Ford that minute, to invite the girls to go berry picking with her.

"News travels fast," remarked Aunt Jane. "How did you know Linda and Susan were here?"

"Heard it on the party line," said Mabel Slocum. She wasn't even embarrassed. "Look, girls, you don't have to pack a lunch. I'll bring fried chicken and things for us all."

Mrs. Slocum was famous for her "fried chicken and things" lunches. They could come with her in her car, she said, or they could ride horseback, perhaps.

"Oh, let's. Let's take horses," begged Susan.

She wasn't really a rider. Once she had tried Blackie for a bit. It would have to be Blackie again—if they went on horseback. Sarah would as soon have stayed at home with the girls. Sooner. But Susan was so eager for another ride. And as for Linda— Well! Before her illness she had loved riding. Since then she hadn't yet had a chance to be on horseback.

"OK," said Sarah cheerfully, and she went to catch and saddle the horses. Robbie's Bayard for Linda—Robbie wouldn't mind. And Blackie for Susan, because she was so gentle and so safe. And that left Wally for Sarah. He was slab-sided and clumsy, but today Sarah was too happy to mind much.

"Do you really think, Linda, darling—" began Aunt Jane, who was worried about her niece.

"We'll be careful," they chorused.

They would not need to carry anything. Besides the lunch, Mrs. Slocum was taking pails for the berries they would pick. "I'll just breeze along," she called as the car turned a tight circle. "You know the place. Down by the river. You follow the old Indian trail."

"Yes, we know," called Sarah and Susan.

"This is the most fun I've had in a long time," said Susan as the girls started down the driveway together. Bayard and Linda looked stylish, thought Sarah. Linda had had riding lessons. She sat straight and always remembered to tuck in her elbows. Sarah rode like a cowboy, and that was no wonder. Keith was her teacher. But Susan—Susan sat like a sack of meal.

In a way, though, Susan got the most fun out of this ride. On account of her they had to go slowly, and if they hadn't had so much fun just talking, it would have been a pokey ride for two of the three. But the sun, the breezes, the birdcalls, the smell of growing things, and most of all, just being together, made them wild with happiness.

"But what's so special with Mrs. Slocum's old saskatoon berries?" asked Linda with a laugh.

"Don't you *like* saskatoons?" said Susan, astonished.

"Not much," admitted Linda. "I had some last summer. They're *sort* of nice, I guess."

"Why, saskatoon pie is the best kind there is," said Susan.

"It's my favorite too," said Sarah. "We always can a lot for pies. But *this* year—"

And the two Braeburn girls explained about the hailstorm that stripped all the fruit trees and shrubs everywhere it struck last spring. Because it missed the Slocums, their wheat would be ready for harvesting long before anybody else's. And they were the only ones who had fruit in their garden and along their river hills.

"It's real generous of Mrs. Slocum to let us pick berries," added Susan. "She might have sold them all and made money. But she's giving them away."

The long, slow, happy miles to the river were easy. But going down the looping hills was a bit tricky, especially for Susan. Every spring the runoff water from the winter snows tore down this old Indian trail, making deeper and deeper ruts. Then in summer the ruts and holes got overgrown with grasses and shrubs. You had to watch carefully where your horse stepped.

Sarah couldn't help feeling anxious about Blackie. A horse needs a good guide, and Susan was no guide at all. But they got down to the river flat safely. And Mrs. Slocum was waiting for them.

The girls would have liked to run down to the water, first thing. Because of the dense screen of trees, they couldn't even see the river from the parking place. But Mrs. Slocum had opened the hamper, and was spreading an old tablecloth on the ground. The river would still be there later.

The girls tethered their horses in a shady place, just out of sight, and took off their bridles. Mrs. Slocum had brought oat sheaves for the horses.

"You think of everything," said Sarah admiringly when they came running back to join her.

"You're a very kind lady," agreed Susan soberly.

"Ah, go on with your blarney. Here, girls, see if you can spread out these blankets."

The girls giggled and tumbled around as they tugged the blankets into place. Everywhere there were awkward little bumps and hollows. Stubborn little shrubs poked up under the blankets, and refused to lie flat.

"We'll just have to squash 'em flat," said Susan, and she plunked down in the middle of the blanket. Still giggling, Sarah and Linda nestled down on either side of her, facing Mrs. Slocum. Between them was the tablecloth and the food. A bowl of fried chicken, still hot in its nest of newspaper, hardboiled eggs, radishes, tiny onions, baby lettuce, buttered rolls, slices of cherry-nut cake, apple tarts. And there was a jug of cold lemonade.

"OK, girls. Dig in," invited their hostess.

The girls looked at each other, and Susan dug her elbow into Sarah's side.

"We—we always pray before we eat," ventured Sarah. She could feel herself getting pink.

" 'Course you do," agreed Mrs. Slocum kindly. "Silly of me not to remember. You just go straight ahead, Sarah."

Afterwards, they dug in, and it was one of the jolliest meals they had ever eaten.

Mrs. Slocum was rather quiet. She usually was such a booming lady. Today she mostly listened to the girls' nonsense, smiling at them. Then, after lunch, she went to sit in the car —and fell asleep! They still sat talking, in half whispers, so as not to disturb.

A year ago, almost, the three of them were together when something wonderful happened. Linda received the Lord Jesus as her Saviour! It happened outdoors, in the meadow at the Scotts' place, during threshing time. They had never really been alone together since that day, so no wonder they were reminded of it.

In one year, you learn a lot about being a Christian. You learn things about your own nature. You learn that often you have to say no when you'd really like to say yes—and you'd better say yes, often, when you feel like saying no. Things seem to go by contraries. It's like going uphill, uphill. When it would be so much easier to roll downhill.

"But you two have each other," said Linda. "You're not climbing the hill alone. In my room in school I guess I'm the only Christian."

This was serious talk, but all the while Linda was busy drawing a funny picture of Mrs. Slocum. She hoped to be an artist when she grew up. Wherever she went, she carried a sketchpad with her, and today she even had some crayons. So she colored Mrs. Slocum's fiery flyaway hair and her freckled face, sagging with sleep. The sketch was funny, but Sarah knew Mrs. Slocum would be tickled with it.

When the drawing was done, Linda tiptoed to the car, and tucked it under the windshield wiper, where Mrs. Slocum would see it the minute she awoke. Then they followed the trail that led to the river.

Standing high on the bank they looked across the broad Saskatchewan River. The name is Indian and means "swift flowing water." There are two branches. This was the north Saskatchewan, wide and swift, with rolling hills on either side.

The water far below winked at the girls. Here and there were sandbars and islands overgrown with trees and shrubs. You could see the current curling around them. Driftwood bobbed past in the rushing water. If you looked steadily at the water, you found yourself swaying. The river surely meant to pull you in!

"A boat's coming!" exclaimed Susan, who had sharp eyes. "Say, I think that's Siddonses' boat! Look, someone's bailing. It's a leaky old tub."

"But isn't it dangerous to row down the river in it?" said Linda.

"Sure, but the Siddonses are reckless people, Ma says. They do a lot of crazy things, but they always come out all right. Like a cat always landing on its feet."

Sarah knew what Susan meant. The Siddonses were squatters. They didn't own land the way other people did. They could, but they didn't. Their home was a shack, and terribly crowded. It didn't *have* to be that way, Father always said. In this country, with the wooded river hills so handy, anybody could chop all the trees he wanted and make a really neat house. But Mr. Siddons never did a lick of work if he didn't have to.

Mrs. Siddons didn't seem to care. Nor the children. There were a lot of them—about 13. Sarah hadn't counted lately. Suddenly she clutched Susan's shoulder. "That's Bertie—your brother Bertie! And Johnny and Archie Siddons."

She was right. Bertie was bailing water with a tin can. He had to work fast to keep up with the leak.

"Oh, Susan, Susan," groaned Linda, in a half-whisper.

Susan's pudgy face had gone white. Maybe the Siddonses always landed on their feet like cats. But it's different, somehow, when your brother is in danger too.

"He can swim," she said. "But the river's dangerous to swim

in because of whirlpools. He's going to catch it from Pa. You just see. He's going to catch it. Yoo-hoo!" she called.

Sarah and Linda joined in. "Yoo-hoo! Yoo-hoo!"

The boys looked up. Bertie was bug-eyed at the sight of Susan. "How did you get here?" he bawled, still bailing away.

For a moment Susan forgot the leaky boat. "I rode," she said proudly. "Horseback. But you're going to catch it, Bertie Gerrick! When Pa finds out you went out in that leaky thing!"

"Aw, can it!" advised Bertie. After that he was too busy to say anything more. The boat lurched out of sight around the bend.

For a moment the girls felt unsettled. But worrying was no good. And they remembered they had come to pick berries. So they ran back to visit with the horses for a bit, then each took a gallon syrup pail from Mrs. Slocum. She had finished her nap, and she knew where all the best berry places were.

For Linda's sake, they kept to the more open spaces. The bushes were low and it meant they had to stoop, but the berries were big and juicy. Before long, the girls had purple fingers and lips. Even Linda. But their lips were busy laughing and talking too.

The mosquitoes weren't too pesky today. A breeze was blowing. That helped. Halfway up the hillside was Mrs. Slocum. Her head was just visible in the middle of a thick saskatoon bush. They saw her wipe perspiration from her face. It must be hot there. And mosquitoey.

The girls' pails filled pretty fast, in spite of all the chatter. In a shady place Mrs. Slocum had placed a four-gallon milk pail. The girls could empty their berries into that every now and then.

The sun beat down. It was thirsty work.

"Let's go back to the car and see if there's any lemonade left," suggested Sarah.

"Yes, let's. No, let's not," said Susan.

"Make up your mind," said Linda, and all three laughed. Everything was funny today.

"What I mean is—there's a spring that comes pouring out of the hillside by the creek. Let's go and drink there."

They left two gallons of berries standing beside the half-filled big one. But Susan carried her empty pail with her. "For Linda," she explained. "She'd better not try climbing down the creek bed. It's slippery."

Sure enough, before long they could hear water running. The path was moist underfoot, and the trees and shrubs grew thicker. Chipmunks dashed and chirped about in hazelnut trees. And there was the creek, its banks all overgrown so you could only guess at how steep they were. Susan, who had been here several times before, knew just where it was safest to climb down. Carefully, she began hopping upstream on stepping stones. The tops of some were under water.

"Ooh, cold!" she squealed as she disappeared behind a screen of dogwood. But not for long. You could hear water running into the pail now, and when she came back, carefully balancing herself, she carried a brimming pail of cold, clear water.

Linda got first chance. She was company. Then Sarah. The edge of the pail pressed her cheeks. She could smell the tin of the pail, but the water was as good as Susan had promised. And cold.

It was nice in the cool shade, and they were tempted to stay. Then they saw the crown of a hill not far away. That and the slope were bare of trees and shrubs. Sarah and Susan looked at each other, and grinned. *Just right for rolling down.* All you had to do to get there was to follow the same cow path.

"Shall we?" asked Susan.

"Yes, let's," Sarah agreed.

"Yes, do," urged Linda. She wasn't going to try climbing the slippery grass, of course. But watching could be fun.

"Race you to the top," called Sarah.

Climbing, slipping, panting, laughing, the two friends made for the top. And they reached it. Looking one way they could see the river. In the other direction were hills covered with berry bushes and trees. Somewhere in there Mrs. Slocum was picking saskatoons. At th foot of the hill Linda sat on a stone, sketching a picture of Susan and Sarah. It was sure to be funny—and good. But just wait till she saw them come rolling!

They lay down on their backs on the grass, their hands clasped on their tummies. Sarah's head pointed north, Susan's south.

"OK, now," said Susan, who always liked to take charge. "One-ah, two-ah, three-ah, go!"

The first moment of a roll is scary. After that you feel grass tickling your face and ears. You see the sun spinning crazily, and the blue sky swooping around. You bounce from elbow to elbow. And suddenly you stop with a thump, and the whole world settles back into place.

Susan and Sarah sat up dizzily.

"You crazy, crazy girls," said Linda, laughing, as she pulled bits of grass out of their messy hair. There was admiration in her tone too.

"Want to try again?" challenged Susan promptly.

"No, not me," said Sarah.

"Me neither. Let's go pick some more berries."

But they dawdled for a bit. Then they heard the car horn. Mrs. Slocum had told them she'd honk when it was time to go.

They couldn't run, on account of Linda. At last they came to the spot where their pails had been. The large pail with berries was gone. When the girls arrived at the car, there stood three big milkpails full of berries. Mrs. Slocum had picked more than twice as much as the three girls!

"Never you mind," she said. "I wanted you to have a good time. As long as you have—"

"Oh, we have, we have!"

"Well, then. That's all that matters."

The girls thought of visiting the horses before they ate a snack, but Mrs. Slocum was in a hurry to get home to do her chores. They ate rather quickly. Then she loaded the berries into the back seat of the Ford, and the car circled away. "Better come along soon," she called back with a look at the sky. "We're in for a thunder shower, or I miss my guess."

They could hear the motor growling up around the steep curves. Sarah and Susan went for the horses. Now, cowpaths are funny things. They wriggle so. This one led over a knoll, and around a bush— The girls stopped to stare. The horses! *Where* were the *horses?* Blankly the girls looked at each other, then they stared all around again. This was the place, wasn't it?

"There's some of the oatsheaves left," said Sarah.

But the horses were gone!

CHAPTER 8

SARAH TAKES CHARGE

THE HORSES hadn't torn their halter ropes. Maybe they hadn't tied the ropes tightly enough, thought Sarah, as her mind skittered around, trying to find some reason why the horses were gone.

"They were tight as could be," said Susan. "I tried them, every one."

And if Susan said they'd been tight, then they were tight. She was always dependable.

"It was those boys," said Susan.

And, of course, it must have been Bertie and Johnny and Archie.

"Just wait till Pa hears about this. Bertie'll catch it," said Susan. "Where'll we *find* the horses, Sarah? What'll we *do?*"

Well, first they tried calling the boys, coaxing and scolding. The woods sent back their shouts. But no boys answered. Then Sarah tried whistling, thinking Wally or Blackie might answer. It's hard to pucker up your lips when you're anxious and angry. But she managed the two long notes that Stuart always used to call the horses when they were at the far end of the pasture.

Then she made shushing motions to Susan. "Listen!"

They stood, straining their ears. But all they heard was a growl of thunder. Oh, dear, what if rain should come pouring down?

Distracted, Susan went galloping back to tell Linda she'd just have to wait alone some more. She and Sarah would have to go in search of the missing horses. Then together they trotted along a path. It was dark here. The whole sky was growing dark. They came to a fork in the path. *Now* what?

Half despairing, Sarah whistled again and again. Then she called, "Blackie! Blackie!"

And Blackie answered. He sounded quite close.

"Those boys!" exclaimed Susan. "They've taken them straight into the bush. See where the plants are broken and stepped on? Just wait till Pa hears!"

Branches whipped their faces. Thorns scratched their arms and legs and faces and caught at their dresses. But in a little hollow they found the three horses, safe. Just when they were untying the halters, thunder rattled overhead again. By the time they had led the horses back onto the path where they could mount, the first raindrops were splatting down.

They'd have to get going. The rutty road to the top of the climb could get awfully slippery when wet. But now it seemed that *Linda* had disappeared. When they called her, there was a far-off answer from the direction of the river. She must have gone for a last look at the water. It was simply pouring now. The horses tossed their heads, snorting. They trampled about, impatiently. It was hard for Sarah to hold all three. Susan had run to hurry Linda along. *Why* didn't they *come?*

When Susan broke into the clearing, shouting Sarah's name,

her eyes were huge in her heated face. "The boys! They're on an island. I think their boat's sunk. Come and see what you think."

This meant tethering the horses once more. The girls ran along the path, all slithery now, to the bank where they stood when the boat came downstream at noon. In the wind and the rain, stood Linda. *She'll catch cold,* Sarah worried. Then she looked to where Linda was looking.

The rain was like a slanting grey curtain now. Clouds had darkened the day early. But there stood three boys, waving a stick with a wet shirt tied to it. Then they dropped the stick, and all three yelled through cupped hands: "HELP! HELP! HELP!"

The girls waved in answer, then they huddled in the shelter of a bush where the rain could not strike so directly. They thought of the treacherous road uphill, and of Susan who had never really been on horseback before today.

"You'd better stay here, Susan," decided Sarah. "Linda and I could get help faster if—"

"I'm staying with Susan," declared Linda. "To keep her company."

"Well, maybe you'd better."

Susan cheered up directly, in spite of the rain. "You take Blackie if you want to," she offered generously.

But Sarah stuck with Wally. He had horse sense. He was surefooted, even if he looked clumsy. His hooves slithered only a few times all the way to the top of the climb. There, he lengthened his stride.

Fortunately the thunder and lightning had moved farther off. Sarah crouched over Wally's back to shield her face from the rain, and she planned what to do. She needed to get to a telephone fast. She'd have to call Susan's Ma—and the Siddonses—but the Siddonses didn't *have* a telephone! Well, then, the Gerricks—or somebody—would have to carry the message. But for several miles of her way there wasn't one farmstead, not till she neared the Slocum driveway.

Wally was stubborn there. He wanted to go straight *home.* But Sarah turned his head firmly, and they trotted up the driveway. Car tracks cut up the mud of the yard. She slipped down, threw the reins over the gatepost, and went running up the boardwalk to the porch. She rapped on the door, then pounded with her fist. No one answered. She looked back over her shoulder. The car shed door stood open. Empty. Still, she kept hoping Mrs. Slocum would be at home. Milking in the barn, maybe? But the cows stood in a wet huddle near the corral gate, waiting for Mrs. Slocum.

Sarah couldn't wait any longer. The door was unlocked, of course. Hardly anyone locked their doors in the country. In the kitchen the pails of berries stood in a row on the table. The grandfather clock ticked solemnly. A tabby cat crawled out from under the stove and rubbed herself against Sarah's wet ankles, mewing. Sarah wasn't very familiar with the house, so she had trouble finding the telephone. At last she found it in the central hallway.

It was dark there, and cool. Sarah shivered as she began cranking the handle. First she called home. She rang and rang. No answer. Then she tried Aunt Jane's. No answer. Where *was* everybody?

Sarah couldn't waste any more time. Back to Wally she ran once more. She urged him to a quick trot, but instead of heading home she took the first corner south. Stuart and Robbie were working the southwest 40 acres today. Maybe—maybe— Oh, good! Through the rain she could see one team close to the corner now. She hoped it would be Stuart.

It was Robbie. He had just finished his job. They met at the corner. Wally shook his head with disgust over having to stand still in the rain, but he stood while Sarah poured out her story.

"And *nobody's* home! Nobody! And we've got to get help. Linda and Susan are there in the rain, getting wetter and wetter, and—"

"Hey, hold on. Pipe down a bit, can't you? Mother and Aunt Jane went to Paxton, that's why they didn't answer. Did you call the Gerricks? Why ever *not*? Just like a girl! You ride to Aunt Jane's— Sorry, I've got to take the team home. Unless you want to change places?" he added hopefully.

"You mean, me take them home and unhitch them and all? Uh-uh! Not me!"

"OK, then. You call the Gerricks. And better try Keith, though I don't suppose he'll be in his house this time of day. And get a wiggle on."

"Oh, you!" said Sarah. But she was glad she had been able to share her worry with someone, even if it was only Robbie.

Out of breath, and dripping worse than ever, Sarah tied Wally to Aunt Jane's gate a few minutes later. Indoors, she crossed the neat, neat kitchen, leaving squishy tracks. She called Central, because Gerricks were on another party line. She could hear the telephone ringing and ringing. *Oh, please, God, let someone be home there. Please, please!*

"Hello! Hello!" It was Susan's ma's voice.

Sarah's was weak with relief. "This is Sarah Scott."

"What's happened? Speak up, Sarah. Where's Susan?"

"She's all right. At least, I think she is. She's down at the river—"

"In this *rainstorm*? Of all things! I might have known! I had a feeling I shouldn't let her go. I'm always so careful with Susan. She catches colds easily, and—"

"Please, *please*, Mrs. Gerrick. Listen!"

"—and most likely she'll be down in bed for a week. And

I'm in the middle of canning vegetables. All the vegetables seem to be ready at the same time this year."

"Please, listen—"

"All the garden stuff to be taken care of, not to mention the cows and chickens, and now, most likely, I'll have to be running the stairs, nursing Susan—"

Sarah clutched the receiver, while Mrs. Gerrick talked and talked. Was nobody going to listen to her?

"Mrs. Gerrick!" growled a man's voice suddenly. "Will you kindly SHUT UP! There, that's better!"

"Well, I never!" gasped Susan's ma.

The man paid no attention to her. "There, little sister. That should hold her for a while. You go right ahead. What was it you was wantin' to say?"

Sarah felt like laughing and crying. Her voice shook, but she told her story as fast as possible.

"Got that, Mrs. Gerrick?" said the man. (Who was he? Sarah didn't recognize the voice.) "Sorry I had to be so rough. But you ladies, once you get to yakkity-yakking—Listen, we better give a line call. Get a party to go down there, see about getting those fool boys off that island."

Dripping and shivering, Sarah still remained glued to Aunt Jane's telephone. *Now* things were happening. Now someone was doing something. In a few minutes, the line call came through—five long rings. Sarah could hear the click-click-click as receivers were lifted for miles around. Central read the announcement: "Three boys are stranded on an island in the middle of the North Saskatchewan river. About three miles north of Carmen Ferry. Anyone owning a boat please get in touch with H. Ferris."

"What boys?" said someone.

"That'll be the Siddonses brood," said someone else. "They're always in mischief, the rascals."

But Sarah knew that in many homes people would be getting ready to go to the rescue. This was like being part of a storybook. She took a long, long breath and raced for the door, not even stopping to wipe up her tracks.

Rain was still falling, but more lightly. Rain didn't matter, she thought. She couldn't get any wetter. She untied patient Wally and got onto his back again. At the half-mile corner he wanted to turn east and go home. But he obeyed Sarah's tug, and they headed west and north again.

Afterward, Mother said, "Why, Sarah? You couldn't do any good down there. Your job was done. Why didn't you come home?"

But Sarah said, "How could I? Linda was down there—and Susan—and Blackie. How could I go home?"

"You had to see the affair to a successful conclusion, did you?" said Father, understandingly.

"At the risk of her health?" said Mother, and she brought out the goose grease to rub Sarah's chest.

But that was afterward. Now Sarah rode, and she was glad the wind wasn't blowing in her face. A car came from the rear. It growled and it swung and it snorted, because of the slithery road. But it caught up with Sarah. At the wheel sat Susan's ma.

"Here, Sarah. Here, child," called Mrs. Gerrick. She was out, and she was holding Wally's bridle. "You poor thing. You're *sopping!*"

When the car drove on again, Sarah was inside, and a prickly wool blanket was wrapped around her, like a cocoon. As for Wally—poor Wally—he was tied to a fence post back there. Sarah had thought of sending him home. But Mother, if she should be home now, would be terribly frightened if he came home without a rider.

Other rescuers arrived at the river ahead of Mrs. Gerrick.

Two cars were parked at the rim of the river hills. Linda and Susan sat in one of them. They came running now, and the three girls snuggled together in the back seat of the Gerrick car. They told Sarah that her brother Keith had brought them up on his horse, Masquerade! A lot of men had gone down the hill. And one car, with a boat riding on its top, had just gone down too. This car had iron chains on its tires to keep it from slithering so badly.

Susan's ma decided to walk downhill—in all the mud and rain. It seemed she simply couldn't wait to make sure Bertie was safe.

She had brought dry clothes for the girls—Susan's clothes. They were rather short and wide for Sarah and Linda. But the girls were glad to wiggle out of the cold, wet clothes into dry ones. Susan's ma had even thought of bringing hot water bottles. The rain tapped on the roof and flapping side curtains of the car. The little oval glass windows misted up. But it was as snug as could be.

Susan and Linda wanted to hear all about Sarah's adventures. And they had to tell what it was like, waiting down at the river for all those hours, though it seemed much longer than it actually was. Waiting is the hardest thing to do. They tried shouting to the boys, but the rain on the river drowned out their voices.

"Know something?" said Sarah suddenly. "This morning I thought this was going to be an ordinary day. But it hasn't been a bit like that."

"It's been *extra*ordinary," said Linda.

"They're coming! They're coming!" squealed Susan, peering through the misty glass. And there they came. The car with the boat on its roof, first of all. And a lot of muddy men, shoving and rocking and lifting the car whenever it was in danger of getting stuck. Bertie was there with them. And

Johnny and Archie Siddons. Then came Keith Scott on Masquerade. He was leading Bayard. And Susan's ma was riding Blackie!

Keith stopped at the Gerrick's car. "Well, Sis, ready to come home with me now?"

Mrs. Gerrick protested. She thought Sarah had better go with her and spend the night with Susan. Linda was going to. But after her ride, Sarah was ready to go home—ready for a hot bath and her own bed.

When she and Keith finally had the horses all safely home, she could think of nothing more wonderful than to go to sleep. But—first came the business with the goose grease. And a cupful of hot milk to warm up her throat. Mother scolded a bit as she rubbed and rubbed Sarah's throat and chest with the grease.

Father stood in the doorway, watching. "Well, Princess, what kind of a day did you have?" he asked.

"Extra—" She yawned. "—Ordinary."

Father chuckled.

Sarah's sleepy thoughts were a jumble—like pictures flicking on and off. Bushes covered with big juicy berries—riding, riding in the rain—nibbling a crisp chicken wing—Bertie Gerrick's face, muddy and sheepish and mischievous—reading *Little Women* down at the creek— Hey, what ever happened to that book! Did she bring it up, or didn't she? Well, if she didn't, it surely would be soaked right through now—telephoning, and that Mr. H. Ferris, whoever he was—he—sure—took—charge—

Sarah slept.

CHAPTER 9

BACK TO SCHOOL

SARAH'S DAY had been rich and lazy. All forenoon, after morning chores, she sat on the bank of the creek, reading. All afternoon, before evening chores, she sat in the shade of the caragana hedge, reading. Twice Mother called out, "Well, Sarah! Haven't you anything else to do? You'll ruin your eyes!" But she didn't say STOP. So Sarah read on. Today's book *Almost as Good as a Boy* was from the school library.

Last week on Monday a lot of Braeburn ladies and girls met at the schoolhouse to clean and air the place. To sweep and dust, scrub and polish. When they left, every windowpane sparkled, and the schoolroom smelled of polish and sweeping compound and soap. Hugging a couple of books under her arm, Sarah took a last look from the doorway before she raced out to the fence post where Blackie was tied. *The room won't stay clean and quiet like that for long!* she thought as she rode homeward.

There'd be a new teacher in Braeburn this year. Every time Sarah thought of that she felt sad—and excited. She would miss Mrs. Grant Millar. Dreadfully. But—the new

teacher had such a lovely storybook sort of name. Cecilia
Wentworth! The very sound of it sent a tingle through Sarah.
She just knew they'd be friends.

There'd be other changes in school. None of last year's
grade eight boys and girls would be back. All of them had
passed their provincial examinations. Their names had been
published in the Paxton weekly! Robbie would be riding or
driving to Blakely every school day to attend high school
there. And Sarah—when winter closed in—would have to
drive the cutter to school by herself. She prickled all over at
the thought. Driving through snowdrifts can be tricky.

But today was summer still. Even while she read on, she
could hear the whirling, rattling hum of two binders that
were going round and round on the wheat field just west of
the house. But her thoughts were following the heroine,
Mabel MacAllister.

"Sarah!"

She jerked. Gradually her eyes came to focus on the porch.
Mother stood there with a basket hanging from one hand and
a gallon pail from the other.

"Care to come with me, Sarah? For the last time this year,
likely. Father hopes to finish cutting the grain tonight."

Sarah slapped her book shut and jumped up. "Wait for me!
Wait for me! I've got to put on my runners."

"Hurry, then." And Mother added, "You're such a book-
worm." But she didn't sound scolding. Everybody in this
family loved reading.

Sarah raced upstairs and came skimming down again a
minute later. Her runners were torn and patched and torn
again. Two toes stuck out. But old runners are better than
walking barefoot through stubble.

At the well, Sarah caught up with her mother, who was
hauling at a rope, hand over hand. Up, out of the cool well,

came a dripping gallon pail. Sarah knew it held ice-cold buttermilk. Sarah carried that. The other pail was hot. It held
coffee.

They cut across the yard. They crawled through the barbed-
wire fence. And then they were on the wheat field. The dry
stubble crunched under Sarah's feet and scratched her ankles
so they bled in places. She looked over the field. The two
binders had begun cutting at the outside edges of the field,
making a wide, wide rectangle at the start. But the rectangles
got tighter and tighter, each time round. Here and there,
where the waving wheat had stood, were teepees or "stooks"
of sheaves, all crowded together.

Stuart, Robbie, and Ivan were doing the stooking. Robbie,
who was farthest away, was the first to spy Sarah and Mother
coming. He cheered, waving his straw hat. Stuart and Ivan
dropped their sheaves. Keith and Father stopped their
binders.

Mother and Sarah headed for a stook near Father's binder.
Everyone chose a sheaf to sit on while Mother unpacked the
basket. Fresh dills; slices of newly baked, warm, buttered
bread; pieces of cheese; and cinnamon buns. And jam-jam
cookies with butterscotch icing between for dessert. And
cups of hot creamy coffee or buttermilk to drink.

"Looks wonderful to me, Mother," said Father as he and
the boys took off their hats to say grace.

There's something special about table grace if you say it
out in the sunshine like this. As if God is closer. A breeze
rustled through the sheaves. A meadowlark was singing his
autumn song. And that minute too, Sarah heard the high, far-
off *kwook-kwook-kwook* of migrating geese. Flying south.
Summer's almost over, they seemed to be calling. It took a
minute for the Scotts to locate the birds, they flew so high,
and you had to look against the sun.

Father wiped his damp curly hair with his red bandana. Sarah noticed the red circle that ran around his forehead where the hatband had pressed. Like a crown!

The Scotts talked about a lot of things while they ate. About the crop. It was late on account of the hail, but it was a good crop. Each time Sarah thought of that, she tingled. Last spring Father promised to buy a car. *If* the crop was good. *If* no frosts came to spoil it. None had.

Lately, Father and Mother had begun to plan a trip by car to visit some relatives in southern Saskatchewan. Just the two of them. As soon as the threshing was done and some wheat sold this fall, they'd get the car—and go! It was a proud thing to think of. Imagine—going about 220 miles in their own car, in one day! By buggy it would take days. By car, if the roads weren't muddy, they could do it in about 10 hours.

"Thatcher stopped by here," said Father. "Pretty down-hearted. He's been overhauling his steam engine. Needs repairs, it seems. Parts have to be ordered from the East. Says it may take two weeks before the outfit is ready to begin threshing again."

"Two weeks!" exclaimed Mother in dismay.

They all knew what she was thinking. There were only about four threshing outfits for miles and miles around. Each fall the machines crawled from farm to farm, to thresh the grain. The farmers and their boys formed the crews. For them, threshing time went on and on. For weeks. Even months, depending on the weather.

This year, because the hail made everything late, they needed to hurry. What if snow came before the fields were cleared? What if all the wheat and oats and barley had to be left outside over winter! One year, snow fell on September 7, and it never went away till next spring. It could happen again. You could never tell.

"Shouldn't we— Hadn't we better switch to the Turner outfit?" said Mother slowly.

"And leave Thatcher in the lurch? Put yourself in his place, Sheila. Would you want others to do that to us?"

Mother sighed. "No, I suppose not. But he should have begun his overhauling earlier!"

"He's had a busy summer like the rest of us," said Father patiently. "As a matter of fact, Thatcher offered to release me from my promise. Several other farmers have withdrawn their business."

"Well, then—"

"It would not be right." Father was very firm. "It would be like kicking a man who is down. You know—I was wondering. What if we should go on that trip now?"

"How?" said Sarah. "We have no car."

Father tweaked her ear. "We'd buy one, of course."

"Without money?" she said. Father didn't believe in going into debt.

He looked over this field—and the next one. Stooks, thousands of stooks, stood—thousands of bushels of grain. A good crop. And if no rain came before it could be threshed, the color would be right—and it would be grade No. 1 Northern.

"I don't think we'd be risking much, buying that car now," said Father, smiling. "But we'll pray about it—seek the mind of the Lord."

The answer must have been Yes, because the car—a 1927 Ford Touring—was delivered to the Scott farm the very next day. Next year's model. That new!

It was Saturday. All day Sarah worked hard. She didn't read the rest of *Almost as Good as a Boy*—not even a snatch. She longed to. But the car was coming in the evening—and all of them were going for a drive. So Sarah rushed through her chores to be good and ready.

She cleaned up her room. She cleaned and polished all the lamps and filled them with oil. She cleaned and polished the family shoes. She dried dishes. She picked all the late peas and beans in the garden and shelled them under the spruce trees, with Bouncer and Ginger fooling around nearby.

Morning and evening she milked a cow. She gathered eggs and packed them in crates. She filled the woodbox with split wood for Robbie, because he was finishing the stooking job today. She washed and ironed her hair ribbon for tomorrow and washed her hair. And she was washing the porch steps when she heard a croaking horn—and her heart jumped in a funny way. Because, there came the car!

Sarah wiped the lowest step fast, and sloshed the water into the grass. There! Then she went running.

"Sarah!" called Mother. "Your dirty dress!"

It *was* a bit messy. And there was a strange man with Father, the salesman from Paxton. But no one was looking at Sarah. Stuart and Robbie had come from the barn. In turn they cranked the car to try the feel of it. They poked their heads under the hood. They examined the brakes and throttle. Sarah shivered with excitement.

The Ford was grey. She'd never seen a grey one before. All the other Braeburn Fords were plain black. Sarah felt the leatherette cushions. Firm. Bouncy. She stuck her hand into the nifty pockets on the insides of the doors. She ran her fingertips across the ridges of the rubber floor mats. Instead of the little oval glass windows that most cars had, this one had celluloid oblongs in the rear and at the sides. They were better, said Mr. Wheeler, the salesman. They wouldn't tear the cloth so easily, and they never broke.

"Well, Sarah, like to go for a spin?" said Father. His eyes shone and there were red spots on his cheeks.

But Mother interrupted firmly. "We'll have supper first.

Care to join us, Mr. Wheeler?" And to Sarah she added in a whisper, "Go change your dress. *Immediately.*"

All the talk at the table was between Father and the boys and Mr. Wheeler. They talked about spark plugs and pistons and exhaust—a lot of strange-sounding words like that.

"Eat, eat," admonished Mother. But for once Sarah wasn't hungry.

After supper, she and Mother got the first chance to go for a drive. Mr. Wheeler sat beside Father who was behind the steering wheel! Mother was as excited as Sarah. Well, Father was excited too. He almost ran into a fence post at the first corner.

"Whoa, Jim, whoa, Jim," he said in his deep voice.

Sarah giggled, but Mother sat with her hands clasped tightly, not saying a single word.

"You're going on a trip next week?" asked Mr. Wheeler. "Good idea. That should certainly give you a lot of practice in driving."

They drove past the Slocums—past the Heathes—past Aunt Jane Bolton's place. They drove past Braeburn school, and right up to the church. This was the road they would take tomorrow morning. Father was getting acquainted with the road.

They went on, making an irregular circle through the district. Past the Gerricks—past Thatchers. And then home. Stuart and Robbie were waiting for their turn.

"How was the drive? Like it, Sarah?" said Stuart.

"Yes! Oh, yes!"

Mother was walking toward the house. "Come, Sarah," she called. "The dishes are waiting."

So they did them—and they talked about the car. It cost $750, and that was a lot of money. They talked about next week's trip. Mother had begun to pack the big suitcase. It hadn't been used since they went to Ontario last fall. Just as Sarah was putting away the last of the dishes, a car came into the yard. Not the new car.

"Mother! Susan's ma is here," called Sarah.

Mrs. Gerrick was striding up briskly.

"Sheila! Sheila!" she called before she got to the door. She came in without knocking. Then she saw Sarah.

"Ah. Well, Sarah! I met the new teacher today. A very attractive person, I must say. Dresses neatly."

Neat. To Mrs. Gerrick, neatness was very important. Sarah almost asked, "Is she as pretty as her name sounds?" If Father were here, he might ask, "Does she have a sense of humor?" He thought a sense of humor was important in a teacher. Next to a sense of fairness. That's what he always said.

Mrs. Gerrick must have had a long conversation with Miss Wentworth. She had a lot of information on the new teacher's aunts and uncles and cousins—what very important people they were. Two were members of Parliament!

"And she's never had a grade eight student of hers fail his finals. Not one. I asked her. Think of that, Sarah. But, Sheila, that wasn't why I stopped by. I wonder, have you heard about Mabel Slocum?" And the two of them moved away into the living room. And closed the door.

Any other day Sarah might have been curious. Any other day she would have noticed that Mother looked distressed when she and Mrs. Gerrick came out of the living room again. Afterwards she remembered that Mother said, "How long?" And that Susan's ma answered, "Six weeks, they say," just before she drove off.

Mother acted strange that evening. Once Father asked her what made her so abstracted. Did she regret that they had ordered the car? Was she doubtful about their going on the trip? She said no to both questions, and asked Father what in the world he could have done with his white shirt with the satin stripes. He needed that for dress-up occasions on their trip.

In their ride that evening, Father and the boys drove clear to Paxton. They dropped Mr. Wheeler at his own house and came back without him. Stuart and Robbie teased Father later about his driving, laughing a lot. Mother didn't even smile. That seemed strange, when you took time to think of it. Once Sarah wondered what the news about Mrs. Slocum could be. She was still the Braeburn lady whom Sarah loved the most—next to Aunt Jane, of course. She was kinder, more unselfish, than a lot of Christians.

The new car pushed any worrying thought aside. They owned a car—a brand new one, with an important sounding horn. They were going to church in it for the first time. Wouldn't people stare!

All the family studied the clouds that morning. What if it rained? The shiny car would get spattered with mud, besides being hard to manage.

At the breakfast table Father prayed a strange prayer. At least it sounded strange to Sarah. "Lord, are we in danger of being earthly minded today? Don't let us be. Guard us from being more excited about *things* than we are about Thee."

Excited about God.

It gave Sarah an important feeling to step into the back seat of the car and sit between Mother and Robbie. There was no sunshine today, and a wet wind was blowing. Stuart snapped the side curtains into place. Everything smelled so new.

When they passed the Slocum place Mother said, "Look, John. They're getting ready to go out. Do you suppose—"

And Father said, "God grant that they'll come to the House of God to seek His face."

That was Bible talk, with old-fashioned words. It didn't seem to fit with a brand new 1927 car!

Sarah was almost bursting with pride when Robbie unsnapped the curtain, and swung open the steel door for her. After a buggy ride, she would have been clammy with cold this morning and her hair all mussed and crinkled by the dampness. Today she felt like a lady. Her hair ribbon was puffy and perky. Her hair hardly needed a touch of the comb in the cloakroom. And everyone was interested in the Scott car, even if it wasn't a sedan with large glass windows all around, like Aunt Jane Bolton's.

When Sunday School began, Sarah looked up at Father, who was superintendent. He led his favorite Sunday School song—"There is sunshine in my soul today—" And Sarah sang. In the class she had to keep alert to answer questions and read Bible verses when Sister Hammond asked her to. But when Brother Hammond began his sermon she could sit back and look at him attentively—and in her secret mind she was riding along at 35 miles an hour on a sunny day with a cool breeze blowing over her—

Suddenly she sat up with a jerk! Brother Hammond was saying, "I wonder—if all our secret thoughts at this moment would become visible and tangible, how crowded would this sanctuary become? Would we see cattle and machinery and household furnishings filling this place which was meant to be a house of prayer?"

And a car—thought Sarah guiltily. She had been doing the very thing Father had prayed against this morning. She was more excited about *things* than about God.

"I'm sorry," she whispered to God. Listening to the sermon was easier after that.

Dinner was earlier than usual, because the Scotts got home faster. So Sarah had a longer afternoon. The others all had a

Sunday nap. Sarah curled up in the back seat of the car with the curtains all snuggly fastened—and finished her book. The ending was exactly right.

Sarah sighed with happiness as she closed it. Tomorrow, school would begin, and she could return two borrowed books—and take out new ones. Or if there were no new ones, she'd take out *Children of the New Forest* to read again. Tomorrow the new teacher would be there—*Cecilia Wentworth*. But tomorrow Father and Mother were leaving on their trip, so—

Everyone at the Scott home got up early that Monday morning. Mother was earliest of all. When Sarah came downstairs, two of Father's shirts were snapping and jumping on the line. It was a breezy morning. Indoors, everything was rush, rush. Mother was heating irons on the stove, packing things in the suitcase, baking cupcakes, and cooking oatmeal for breakfast.

Besides her own school lunch, Sarah had to pack one for Robbie to take to Blakely. He was starting high school today. Everybody was so busy doing so many things, they hardly had time to sit down together at the table.

Sarah was late in starting for school. She waited only long enough to wave good-bye to Father and Mother. Before they turned the first corner, she was racing toward the barn to saddle Blackie. She was wearing her new blue gingham dress and a blue sweater over it. And a brand new pair of runners. She carried a new slate, new slate pencils, and a box of paints in her new shoulder schoolbag. Behind the saddle she fastened an oatsheaf. Father hadn't had time to take any feed to the school yet, and it seemed cruel to let Blackie stand all day without anything to eat.

But the oatsheaf was a mistake. Usually Blackie was the best mannered lady horse you could find. The rustling oats made her skittish. She turned and turned in circles on the road, trying to find out what the bothersome sound was all about.

"Blackie! You *behave!*" scolded Sarah.

Finally Blackie settled into a bouncy trot, and each bounce said, I don't *like* that thing! Sarah was a quarter of a mile from school when she heard the bell ringing.

A strange thing was happening. All the boys and girls, from the biggest to the littlest, were lining up outdoors! Why, Braeburn *never* marched in when school was called in the morning. But this must be the way Miss Wentworth liked to have it. And, oh, dear, oh dear! Sarah was going to be late. For the second time in her life! The biggest boys and girls were marching up the steps when Sarah galloped into the school yard.

Even though she was late, there were things she had to do. She unsaddled Blackie in the barn, took off the bridle, tied the halter rope. She tossed the oatsheaf into the manger and slipped off the twine. Then, with her bag in one hand and her lunchpail in the other, she raced for the school.

The new teacher was having roll call. "Present—present—present—present—" High tones, low tones, shy whispers from beginners, loud sassy answers from some of the big boys—

"Sarah Scott?" said Teacher's voice.

In the hall, Sarah dropped her lunchpail with a clang and opened the schoolroom door. She was breathing fast.

"P-present," she said.

"S-so y-you are p-present, are you?"

Shocked, Sarah stared at her new teacher. About 25 boys and girls were staring at her. But Sarah had eyes for the teacher only.

She was pretty. She looked smart and dressed-up as could be. Her lips were curved, but her eyes weren't smiling, exactly.

"Is this what you call being present? I would not advise you to be *present* after this fashion. No, I really wouldn't advise it, Sarah Scott."

"I'm s-sorry." Sarah was hot and embarrassed. She couldn't help stammering again. "Wh-where sh-should I sit?"

"I believe Susan Gerrick has saved a place for you. Is that right?" Teacher's face grew kind as she looked at Susan.

Sarah quickly slipped in beside her friend. She emptied her schoolbag. Her hands shook and her eyes felt hot. Teacher spent most of the first period finding out who was who and in what grades they were and whether or not they had the right readers.

It was a strange morning. Teacher was new. The boys and girls were wound up tight as fiddle strings. Mrs. Millar had always allowed them to whisper if it had anything to do with lessons. Now everbody was supposed to raise his hand and ask Teacher. Even if all you wanted to know was which page you were to study.

When recess came, all the older pupils, grades five to eight, gathered in a huddle on the ball field. And they talked about Teacher. Almost everyone felt grumpy.

"She can go right back to Halifax," growled Archie Siddons, who was one of the new grade eights.

"Is that where she came from?"

"Don't know. Don't care. But that's where I'd like to send her."

"Why?" Susan Gerrick wanted to know.

"Because it's far away. The farther the better."

And then Bertie Gerrick, who could imitate people's voices, said, "I wouldn't advise it," sounding like Miss Wentworth. And everybody howled with laughter..

Except Sarah. She felt bewildered. Always—she and her teacher had been friends. Sarah loved to study, even if she wasn't awfully good at learning facts, like dates in history. But she remembered events. Mrs. Grant Millar always said that *how* and *why* and *where* things happened and to *whom* —were more important than knowing exactly what day or month or year they happened.

When the bell rang, Sarah went indoors with the others. Teacher gave a lecture first thing. She had been watching them. It wasn't *healthy* to stand around on the school yard during recess. After this, they would use the break for the purpose for which it was intended. They would *play*. Get exercise. There must be full participation.

"I wouldn't advise you to disregard this request. No, I really wouldn't advise it."

Bertie snorted. Then he pretended he had only meant to blow his nose. But there were a lot of broad smiles in school.

"Take out your reading assignment," said Miss Wentworth sharply.

Sarah cheered up. Reading was her favorite subject. "Grade five, turn to the first poem, on page 9. Prepare for class recitation."

Rule Britannia was the title. Sarah skimmed through it. Every year she was thrilled to get her new reader. Next to the poem was a story, *The Moonlight Sonata*. It looked awfully interesting. Soon Sarah was lost in it—reading about this famous composer, Beethoven, and how he came to compose a famous piece of music. About a poor blind girl who loved music so much, and she—

"Grade five, come forward," broke in Miss Wentworth.

All six of them came to stand in front of the desk.

"Sarah Scott, read the poem please."

She read it—with expression—and looked up hopefully.

"Class, what does the poem suggest to you?" said Teacher.

Susan Gerrick nibbled the insides of her cheeks. Veronica

Siddons shuffled her feet. Nobody knew what to answer. So Sarah spoke up.

"It sounds awfully braggy, doesn't it?"

"Sarah Scott!" Teacher's words came in a shocked whisper.

"Well, what I mean—" Sarah could feel herself turning pink, and she talked fast. "It says that no one else is so happy, and everyone in all the world will envy Britain, and it will get stronger and stronger, and—"

"That will do," said Teacher gravely. "Who has been teaching you to despise our mother country?"

"Sarah's Scotch," said someone.

"I don't despise Britain. Only—"

"That will do. Susan, please read the poem."

That's the way things went. *All* day *long!* Sarah couldn't understand it. The more she tried to do things *right*, the more she found that they were all *wrong*. At least, Miss Wentworth seemed to think so.

"How was school today?" asked Stuart the moment Sarah got home. And, "How was school?" said Robbie first thing when *he* rode up on Bayard. "How's Ivan getting along?"

"He doesn't let any of the big boys tease the little ones," reported Sarah, glad he had changed the subject.

"Hey! Good for Ivan!" said Robbie as he rode away to the corral to turn his horse loose. Sarah took a long breath. Maybe her brothers would forget to ask any further questions. Maybe she and everyone could simply forget that today ever happened.

But Monday was only the beginning of a troubling week. School was not a happy place for Sarah. It was partly her fault.

On Tuesday, during the singing period, Miss Wentworth wanted everybody to sing soprano. Sarah piped up eagerly, "But Mrs. Millar taught us to sing in parts, Miss Wentworth."

"*I* am teacher here, remember. *Not* Mrs. Millar!" said Teacher.

On Wednesday, Sarah rushed through her history assignment—all about the signing of the Magna Carta. Then she took out her library book *The World of Ice* to read. It was full of icebergs and ships, of Eskimos and dog teams and kayaks. It told about a long winter night, and about harpooning whales. Suddenly Teacher's hands reached over Sarah's shoulder, closed the book, and took it away.

"What is the meaning of this?" she demanded. "Is this the way to study history?"

"B—but I know the lesson," said Sarah desperately. Oh, she hoped Teacher wouldn't take the book away. But she did. She placed it in a drawer in her desk.

"Grade five," she called. It wasn't their turn. And when they were all lined up, "All right, Sarah Scott, *when* was the Magna Carter signed?"

Dates. Oh, dear! Sarah never could remember dates. "It was at Runnymede," she said. "That's near Windsor castle. King John was an awfully wicked king, the wickedest one of all. He even *murdered* his nephew, Arthur, who ought to have been king. The barons of England got tired of his wickedness, and they made him sign this big paper, and—"

"Sarah, *when* was it *signed?*"

"I—don't—remember—"

"Susan?"

"June 15, 1215," said Susan, easy as easy.

On Thursday Sarah was caught whispering. Actually, Susan Gerrick began it. In the middle of arithmetic, Susan nudged Sarah. "Do you know about Mrs. Slocum?" she asked.

"No. What?"

"She's got a sickness in her blood. A bad kind."

"Susan! No!" But before she could say anything more

Teacher's voice broke in. "Sarah? Whispering? You'll please remain indoors during recess."

Susan put up her hand. "It was my fault, Miss Wentworth. I began it."

"All right then, both of you remain indoors." And when recess came, she told them to study the exports and imports of the West Indies. And she stayed at her desk to make sure they couldn't talk to each other.

Sarah was sad. Partly because school was such a dreary place now. Partly because she was worried about what Father and Mother would say. *No* Scott was ever punished before in school. Not a single one! Mostly she was sad because of what she had just heard. She remembered Mrs. Gerrick's visit last Saturday. She remembered that Mother asked, "How long?" and that Susan's ma said, "Six weeks."

Only six weeks to *live?*

She understood one thing now that puzzled her last Sunday. Instead of going to the evening service in church, Father and Mother had walked over to the Slocums for a visit. They had never done such a thing before.

Teacher reached for her bell. Recess time was over. "All right, Sarah, what are the imports and exports of the West Indies?"

"I'm—I'm sorry. I don't know them—yet."

But Susan could simply rattle them off. She memorized *facts* so easily.

At noon Sarah heard the rest about Mrs. Slocum. It was true. The doctor said last week that she couldn't live more than six weeks. About five weeks now. And Mrs. Slocum was Sarah's friend!

CHAPTER 10

IVAN TO THE RESCUE

THE NEWS about Mrs. Slocum gave Sarah a numb feeling, a nothing feeling. As if her heart and brains were freezing.

After lunch on Thursday was Composition hour for the whole school. Miss Wentworth gave them a list of titles to choose from. One was *My Friend*. Sarah took that, and she wrote about Mrs. Slocum. Not about the leukemia. She couldn't bear to think about that. She remembered all the kind things Mrs. Slocum did for her, and she put her remembering down on paper. She had to write fast to get it all down in one period. Her heart beat fast when Teacher picked up her scribber to take home with the rest. She was sure it was a good story.

Friday morning the compositions were back. Sarah had a big 65 on hers. *Sixty-five!* Susan got 90%. Her title was "My Summer Holidays." And it began, "I like summer holidays. I like them because I can work in the house and in the barn and in the garden. I help my mother take care of the chickens. I feed the calves. I weed the garden—" That's the way it went. Facts. A lot of facts. *Ninety percent!*

"I want to contrast two papers," said Teacher. She held up Susan's scribbler. "Look how beautifully neat this one is. Susan uses only words she thoroughly understands, words she knows how to spell. There is not a single spelling mistake on the page, not a single smudge. Now, class, look at this page." And she held up *Sarah's* page. It was blotched with red ink.

Teacher had scribbled notes here and there. "Never use words you do not know the meaning of," said one. ("I *don't*," whispered Sarah, indignantly.) "Why don't you try to be neat?" said another. ("I *do*," thought Sarah, growing more and more unhappy.) "Remember, you are a child. Do not try to write like an adult. A child would not have a friendship with an old woman," said a third. "It's unnatural."

"Why's she always picking on you?" growled Bertie Gerrick at noon.

"I—don't—know." Sarah felt too discouraged to cry.

Time crawled that afternoon. It just went inching along like a big hairy caterpillar. After recess was Literary Society time, and everyone was supposed to recite, or tell a joke or a story, or ask riddles, or sing a song. Sarah chose a baby poem to read. (You mustn't use words too big for you!) Her turn came toward the end of the program. And she didn't care how she read it.

"Lifeless, lifeless—" commented Teacher. "Here, I'll show you—" And she was going to read the poem all over again. But someone stumbled to his feet with a startling clatter. "Teacher?"

"Yes, Ivan?"

Everyone was open-mouthed with astonishment. Maybe Ivan was the most astonished of all. But he did not sit down again, though he clutched his desk front with both hands so the knuckles turned white. "I don't like you always talk, talk

so angry to Sarah Scott. She is a nice girl. I—I wouldn't advise it."

There was a stunned silence. Teacher's mouth hung open. Then Bertie Gerrick snorted. That started it. The big boys were laughing, not caring how much noise they made. The little ones sat frightened and quiet. Teacher's face turned a dark red.

"I—I wouldn't advise it," repeated Ivan with an unhappy gulp, and slowly he slid back into his seat.

"*Sit down!* You had better, Ivan Chernishenko!" said Teacher. "When I need your advice I'll ask for it. Class, put away your books. Turn! Stand! Class dismissed!"

Usually now they marched out after school just the way they marched in in the mornings. This time Teacher made a scattering motion with both arms.

The pupils scattered. The big boys pushed down the aisles and through the door. Outside they hooted with laughter. "Ivan, Ivan! How about that, Ivan?!" they shouted, slapping his back. "*I wouldn't advise it*" someone crowded. "*I really wouldn't advise it.*"

While Sarah nervously packed her school bag, she stole a look at Miss Wentworth. She stood straight and stiff, and her face had grown white. Like paste. By the time Sarah had saddled Blackie, everyone else had disappeared. She remembered that this was Friday, and she hadn't taken out any library book for the weekend. *The World of Ice* was still in Teacher's desk. She wouldn't touch that without permission. But the schoolhouse never was locked, nor the bookshelves. If Teacher had left—

The door still stood open. Could Miss Wentworth be there yet? Sarah whispered to Blackie to stand. She tiptoed up the porch steps. Quiet. Then she heard two tiny sounds. She peeked around the door frame. *Teacher was crying.* Her head was down on her arms on the desk, and her shoulders were shaking. Sarah stole back out and down the stairs. She led Blackie out of the yard before mounting. She felt shaky as could be.

A half mile from school, where tall poplars shaded the road, and a ditch full of tall grass invited her, Sarah tethered Blackie to a post. On a large rock she sat and brooded. Over what she had just seen. Over today's troubles, piled on top of the whole week's troubles. Why had so many things gone wrong like this?

"Well, if this isn't my friend, Sarah Scott," said a pleasant voice. And there, looking down at her, was Grant Millar. Sarah was glad to see him, even if he asked the usual hard question.

"How's school?"

"Not—good," admitted Sarah with a sigh.

"What seems to be the trouble?"

Grant Millar was safe. He wouldn't gossip. Besides, every home in Braeburn would be talking about school this evening. Sarah hadn't told a thing to Stuart and Robbie. Now she spilled everything, all her hurt and bewilderment, to this kind friend with the bushy eyebrows and the big heart.

"We all loved Mrs. Millar *so much*," sighed Sarah.

"Don't blame you." He grinned. "But that could be your trouble. Perhaps you're not ready to love another teacher."

"She won't *let* us love her!" objected Sarah. "With Mrs. Millar—" Sarah's eyes grew dreamy. "With Mrs. Millar we could find out things for ourselves. Exciting things. And we could tell her about them, and then *she* got excited. And it was like—like a voyage of discovery together."

"And now?"

"I feel all the time as if Miss Wentworth is trying to *sque-e-e-ze* me into a tiny little box. And I don't fit in!"

He smiled. "Feel better now that you've talked it all out? I'll have to go back to work, I'm afraid. Don't sit here all weekend. I wouldn't advise it."

His eyes twinkled, and Sarah giggled. For the first time in *days.*

She felt lighter while riding home. Loads lighter. The sun was shining on the miles of fields, all golden and brown. Thousands of stooks were waiting to be threshed. They looked like miniature teepees. The ditches were full of goldenrod and wild asters. The air was full of a humming sound. This was autumn, and in its way autumn could be as lovely as spring or summer.

Sarah rode past the Slocum farm. It didn't matter what Miss Wentworth thought. She and Mrs. Slocum were friends, and she took Sarah to town with her and brought piles of groceries and paid for them herself. It seemed strange that she should be so ill now. *Only five weeks more.* And Sarah wasn't sure Mrs. Slocum was a Christian.

When you thought of her kindness, you thought, *How can she not be one?* But kindness doesn't make you a Christian. Only one thing does. You have to be born into God's family. Jesus Himself said so. He said it to a *very good man*—Nicodemus. Straight out He said, "You have to be born a second time, or you will never see the kingdom of God." And *then* He explained that you are born again when you truly believe that Jesus died for your sins, in your place.

He has done it for everyone. But the gift isn't yours until you accept it.

Has Mrs. Slocum ever? wondered Sarah wistfully.

The school trouble crowded in on Sarah again that evening. Ivan came to visit Robbie. Soon as Sarah saw him she knew he'd stir up trouble. He and Robbie played ball in the yard. When he had gone, Robbie knew everything Ivan knew.

And Robbie told Stuart and Keith, who was having supper with them. That supper would have been a jolly time if it hadn't been for Miss Wentworth. Miss Crosspatch, Robbie called her.

"Hey, watch it," said Stuart. "That's no way to talk about Sarah's teacher."

"Well, she *is* a crosspatch. Wish she was a man! I'd go and knock some sense into her—him."

Sarah felt a thrill of pride. Robbie didn't usually stick up for her like that. But with the pride there was a sickish feeling too. She remembered Miss Wentworth sobbing.

Sunday was a difficult day for Sarah. She had known it would be. All Braeburn knew of the trouble in school. In every home people were talking about her. Some looked at her with a "You poor child" look. Others seemed to be saying, "You pert thing! What's the younger generation coming to?" Bertie Gerrick was worst of all. He was with a crowd of boys on the porch steps. When she passed he said, "Hello, nice girl!" and all the boys laughed.

Brother Hammond spoke about an interesting Bible verse. "Quit yourselves like men. Be strong." *Quit yourselves* didn't make much sense. But Brother Hammond explained that was an old-fashioned way of saying, "*Behave*. Behave like men. Show some backbone!"

"That's like Stuart," thought Sarah, remembering last night.

After supper he took her for a long ride, down to the river. They sat on a rock, still warm from the sun, and talked.

"Sarah, have you invited Jesus into your school troubles?" he asked.

"I—I've *prayed* about them. At first I asked God to make Miss Wentworth love me. But that didn't help. So yesterday I asked Jesus to help *me* love *her*."

"How are you going to do it?"

"I don't know," said Sarah, perplexed. "I *don't* love her. How'm I going to *make* myself love her?"

"It can't be done," said Stuart.

Well, then! Sarah's heart lifted. If it was impossible, then she needn't try.

But Stuart wasn't done. "Does Jesus love Miss Wentworth, do you think?"

"Sure." Sarah looked at him in astonishment.

"Sure?"

"Of course. He loves *everybody*."

"And He lives in you."

For a long time Sarah stared at the sunset. Orange and gold and purple lights touched the clouds out there. And a light was slowly growing in Sarah's heart. "Then I—don't have —to do it. I just have to let Jesus love her."

"That's right. It's like handing yourself over to God for the purpose. Like telling Him, 'Here I am, Lord. Fill me with Your love.'"

For a long minute they were silent.

"I've done it," whispered Sarah.

"Good." They squeezed hands then.

That was yesterday, and today Sarah felt entirely different about Miss Wentworth.

After the meeting something surprising happened. The Grant Millars were in church, and they asked Sarah to come and spend the afternoon with them. The weather was so lovely, they ate dinner outdoors. A lame crow and a tame chipmunk begged for food. A friendly pup, a brother of Bouncer Scott, waved his tail between the chairs and among the cups. Mr. and Mrs. Millar and Sarah had a lot of fun over their picnic meal.

Afterward they went for a stroll. Several times Sarah had heard Grant Millar tell about the birds and animals that lived on his farm. Today he introduced her to them. All the wild things knew and trusted him. Birds came to sit on his head and shoulders, to eat out of his hand. Down at the creek, beavers were building a dam. Sarah saw them hug armloads of mud to their chests, and waddle down to plaster it on their house of sticks. It didn't seem to bother them that people were watching. This was like walking through a storybook.

Then Sarah and Mrs. Millar took off their shoes and stockings and went up the creek, hopping from stone to stone. It was the very same creek that wound all through Keith's horse ranch and Sarah's home place. It made a wide loop all through Braeburn. That was where the school and church got their name in the first place. Brae is Scottish for bank or slope. Burn is Scottish for little river or stream. Sarah had known this for a long time. Most of the early settlers in the district had come here straight from Scotland.

"Let's sit down," suggested Mrs. Millar. So they sat down on the grassy brae. Sarah half-expected her former teacher to ask questions about this past week. And she did. Then she said,

"I'd like to tell you a story."

It was a true story, she said. It took place in Saskatchewan. Once upon a time there was this poor girl. Her mother had belonged to a rich, important family. But when she married a homesteader, none of her grand relations would have anything more to do with her. The family had hard times—crop failure, cows dying, sickness—things like that.

But the girl was ambitious. From early childhood she dreamed of becoming a teacher. She worked hard and saved all the dollars and quarters she possibly could. In high school she stood at the head of her class. And by and by she had enough saved to be able to go to Normal school to learn how to teach. And she got her certificate!

Then hard things began to happen again. First, the girl's father was killed in an accident. Then her mother took sick. For 12 years she was in bed, slowly dying. The girl put aside her plans. She stayed home to take care of her mother. She kept the farm going. She plowed and harrowed and seeded the land. Then her mother died.

The daughter wasn't young any more—but she still had her dreams. So she sold the farm and machinery. They weren't worth much. And she went back to Normal school for a refresher course. Then she applied for a school.

"Can you guess which school?" said Mrs. Millar.

"Braeburn?" said Sarah slowly.

"That's right."

Miss Wentworth. And all her important relatives hadn't done her a bit of good. She'd said no single Grade Eight pupils had ever failed their finals! Of *course* not. She hadn't had any! It was like telling fibs.

"I don't see why she has to pretend," said Sarah.

Mrs. Millar laughed. "I'm afraid Grant and I agree with you there. But she says she's thought things through, and this is the way they're going to be. She says she couldn't bear to have everyone asking curious questions about her."

Sarah sat pounding her bare heel into the grass. She thought about Susan's ma—and some other ladies—and she could see what Miss Wentworth meant. Quite probably the teacher would never have mentioned those important relatives if someone hadn't done some prying.

"But why did you tell me?" asked Sarah.

"Grant thought it would help you to see her side of things. This past week has been a rough beginning for her as well as for you."

She made it rough, thought Sarah, and some of the sore feeling came back.

"She's new. She has a lot to learn," said Mrs. Millar. "She's a brave person, but she'll need your help. Yours most of all. If things at school don't improve, there's no telling what may happen. If she has to leave Braeburn, she may be *finished* as a teacher."

She's afraid I'll bear a grudge and make things rough for Miss Wentorth, thought Sarah. And, if it hadn't been for her talk with Stuart last night, maybe she *would* have.

"I haven't done anything to make things difficult," Sarah defended herself.

"Nothing?"

"We-ell—" First Sarah pouted. Then she grinned slowly. "I read *World of Ice* when I should have been memorizing what day that Magna thing was signed."

"What day was it?" asked Mrs. Millar, laughing.

"JUNE 15, 1215!" shouted Sarah. "I'll never, never forget it now."

"Well! So *some* good has come out of this week."

"But what's the use of knowing the day?" grumbled Sarah. "*You* never cared about dates, much. And in reading, you thought expression was important. And you let me have ideas, and talk about them. And you liked me to like new words. And in Composition you thought the story was more important than neatness and spelling. I always got high marks. Know what I had this week—65%! Susan got 90!"

"Think of it this way," suggested Mrs. Millar. "All these years you've been getting higher marks in certain subjects than Susan, though she worked as hard and faithfully as you. Perhaps it's her turn to shine. Will you be able to take it as sweetly as she has—having your best friend stand first in class?"

It was a sober girl who went hopping from stone to stone, down the creek again, back to the Millars' place. Secrets could be bothersome. She knew something now about Miss Wentworth that she mustn't tell anyone. "Except your parents," said Mrs. Millar. They would be safe. She had promised to try to make things easier for Miss Wentworth. *If she'll let me*, thought Sarah.

CHAPTER 11

WHAT SARAH LEARNED

WHEN MONDAY came Sarah was happier about returning to school than she had thought she could possibly be. She was sort of curious. A lot of other pupils must have been too. How would Miss Wentworth act?

She didn't mention Friday at all. She didn't talk at Sarah any more. And she didn't keep repeating, "I wouldn't advise it." But she still liked facts better than imagination. She still thought every single pupil could learn to write neatly if he really tried.

That was Sarah's biggest problem in school now. She tried—she really did. But somehow her papers never turned out the way she wanted them to. The "nice girl" business didn't bother her for long. Bertie said, "Hello, nice girl." *Once.* Sarah smiled right back and said, "Hello, pretty boy."

"Hey!" He looked alarmed. "Don't you start something, Sarah Scott."

"I won't—if you won't," promised Sarah.

And that's how her nickname died. Bertie himself shushed anyone who ever tried to use it. Sarah was safe.

But school was dreary, though perhaps this wasn't Teacher's fault. The whole *world* seemed dreary. Yet the sun shone every day. Here and there you could see crews at work in the fields. The thousands of stooks were disappearing fast, and many fields had strawpiles now. You could see them growing.

You could see men throwing sheaves up on top of a heap of other sheaves on a hayrack. The loads grew higher and higher. Last of all, the men tossed their forks up, then climbed up the side to sit in a nest of sheaves. They grasped the reins, and clucked to their horses, and the little mountains on wheels moved off to the waiting machine. It was greedy. It *gulped* sheaves. It blew out mountains of straw. It spit out the rustling reddish-brown wheat.

This was threshing time, an exciting time! Yet, riding to and from school, Sarah watched the activities with sadness in her heart.

Part of this may have been because Father and Mother were away and the Thatcher machine still wasn't running and the Scott grain wasn't being threshed. The weather was so perfect—and their grain *wasn't being threshed.* Sarah felt left out.

But that was only part of the trouble. The thought that kept running through her head was, *Everything is dying.* Summer. The wheat fields. The trees, shedding their leaves like that. They looked naked and dead. And all the birds were leaving. The air wasn't bubbling with songs any more. It was dead too, sort of.

But that wasn't all. Mrs. Slocum was dying. In school they talked about her. How thin she was getting to be. How awful she looked. What doctors were doing to her. All Braeburn mothers had been to see her. "Ma says—" "Mother says—" At recess the girls—big and little and middle-sized—buzzed with horrified whispers. They *liked* talking about every single dreadful detail. Sarah felt like holding her ears—like saying, "Oh, *be quiet. Please!*"

"They've got a hired girl now. She's Mr. Slocum's second cousin. Her name's Lizzie Drummond—"

"They say her ankles are *bleeding.* Her blood is so thin—" Buzz-buzz-buzz—

There was no way for Sarah to forget. Morning and evening she rode past the Slocum driveway. Usually now several cars were parked in the yard. *She's dying—she's dying. Everybody is going to die. And we don't know when or how. Father, Mother, everybody.* Sometimes Sarah felt she couldn't *bear* it.

When Sarah was alone at home the house had a hollow sound. Stuart was away, helping the Turner crew with their threshing job. He came home only at night. Morning and evening, Robbie did the chores with Sarah's help. But even when she had finished milking her cow, she stayed in the barn rather than go into the whispering house.

This evening she sat in an empty manger, dangling her feet. Robbie was feeding the horses. He would come carrying a big forkful of feed, slap the rump of a horse, pass between two teammates, and drop the feed into the manger. The horses' strong teeth crunched the straw. It was a comforting sound. Sarah needed comfort.

"Hey, what are you mooning about?" Robbie wanted to know.

"Robbie, what's it like to die?"

"*What?*"

"What's it like to die?"

"What's got *into* you? How would *I* know? I've never done it."

"No, but you're going to. And I'm going to. Everybody is. Sure as you're born."

"Well, sure. But it doesn't help any to get all moony about it."

So—it was no use to ask Robbie about these things. And there was nobody else. Keith—? Well, Sarah's big brother was fun to joke with. But he wasn't the serious, talking kind. And Stuart was up long before Sarah was awake and came home long after she was in bed. She never saw him at all now.

Wednesday, she heard him coming home. She'd been lying awake, thinking—thinking. *I've got to die. One day I've got to die. Everybody and everything is dying*— Over and over the thoughts ran through her mind.

The moon shone into her room. It made a ghostly path across the floor to her bed. Sarah shrank away from it, but she stared into the brightness.

There was a light tap on her door. Then it opened a crack. "*Sarah?*" It was the merest whisper.

She sat up. "Is that you, Stuart?"

"Right, first guess." His head poked around the door. Sarah had never been more glad to see anyone. He was still in his threshing overalls, and he smelled of chaff and oil and sweat. It smelled *wonderful*. Not ghostly at all. He came to sit on the edge of her bed.

"What's wrong, Princess? You aren't sick, are you? You've got Robbie worried, let me tell you." Stuart's hand felt her forehead. "No fever."

"I'm not sick," said Sarah. "Really, I'm not. It's only—" And then she poured out to Stuart all the things that bothered her. How she felt and why she felt that way. Stuart was easy to talk to. He was a good listener.

He knew what to answer too.

"It's true that everybody must die—except the Christians who will be in the world when Jesus comes to snatch them away to heaven! *That* could happen just any time! But anyway, death is nothing to fear—for a Christian. Jesus will be right there, all the time!"

Stuart knew all the right verses—a lot of them. "Let not your heart be troubled— In my Father's house are many mansions— I will come again, and receive you unto Myself; that where I am there ye may be also—" And, "Yea, though I walk through the valley of the shadow of death, I will fear no evil— *for Thou art with me*—" And, "Because I live, ye shall live also—" And, "Death is swallowed up in victory."

Because Jesus rose from the dead! Because of that no one who believes in Him need ever, ever be afraid of death! There's heaven. There's a forever-after life in heaven—with no more sin, no sickness, and no more dying.

Now the moonlight wasn't ghostly. It was bright silver, and in its light Sarah knelt beside Stuart, and they told Jesus all about her fears. It was like rolling a big boulder off her shoulders.

When they rose, Sarah gave Stuart a tight hug. She sniffed at his shirt. "You smell like a thrasher."

He laughed. "Well, this thrasher had better get some shut-eye. Four o'clock comes awfully early."

The next day, on the way home from school, Sarah was riding slowly past the Slocum driveway, when a strange lady stopped her. She must have been waiting for Sarah.

"You the Scott kid?" she asked.

"I'm Sarah Scott."

"Well, Mabel wants to see yeh. Bad. Yeh don't mind stoppin' in?"

"N-no." Sarah felt funny though. She had never seen a very sick person. But this was her friend, Mrs. Slocum. Her guide must be that Lizzie Drummond she'd heard about in school. She plodded up the driveway ahead of Sarah and Blackie. Sarah's heart thumped.

Lizzie waited for Sarah to tie Blackie to the gate. Then she led the way indoors. Through the kitchen and into a dark little bedroom. "I've brought the kid, Mabel," she announced. And she left them alone together.

Sarah's heart went on thumping. "H-hello, Mrs. Slocum," she said timidly.

"Well, Sarah," it was a whisper. And Mrs. Slocum had always had a booming voice. "So you've come. I sorta—had a notion—I'd like—to ask you—a question."

Oh, dear! Sarah thought *If only Mother were here!*

"Remember—the day—we picked saskatoons?" Mrs. Slocum asked. Then slowly, she told how she had heard Sarah and Linda and Susan talking. They thought she was napping. They had talked in whispers about what it meant to be a Christian. She had heard.

"Done a lot—of thinkin'—" she said. "A lot—of thinkin'. Always thought—I was—all—right. Now—I'm scared—scared to—die!"

And now suddenly Sarah's heart jumped for joy! "You don't have to be. Oh, Mrs. Slocum, you don't have to be," she broke in eagerly. Because of Stuart, she knew which verses to say.

This was the last time Sarah saw her friend. Next morning they took her to the hospital. In the evening Sarah's parents came home from their trip. There was so much to tell and to listen to. But one of the first things they did was to drive to the hospital in Paxton to visit their sick neighbor.

"How was she?" whispered Sarah when they got back.

Mother had wet eyelashes, but she was smiling. "Resting in Jesus," she said. "She knows at last that she is a child of God—and she knows she will be seeing Him face to face soon. She's not afraid. Sarah—Sarah—how wonderful that you could have a share in bringing her to Jesus!"

"But mostly it was Stuart," admitted Sarah.

Threshing time came with a bang to the Scott place. This year the Thatcher machine was coming here first of all. That was because Father didn't leave him in the lurch, Mr. Thatcher said. It meant that Mother had to get ready in a big hurry. And this year Sarah's sister Kathleen wasn't here to help.

But there was the new Ford Touring car! Father took Mother to Blakely—and they came back with loads of food and cups and things. Aunt Jane would do many of the sit-down jobs—stripping feathers off butchered chickens, peeling vegetables, and slicing apples for pie. Because of her accident last fall, she still had to be careful.

And Sarah? Sarah had to herd cows. *Again!*

Last year that was her job at threshing time. This year she had hoped and hoped she could help by running errands for Mother. It was more fun to be right in the middle of the excitement. But the wire fences had to be lowered so the threshers could drive from field to field easily. If the cattle got into the field of oats they'd do a lot of damage. They might even overeat—and *die*. Father couldn't bear the idea of shutting them up in the barn all day in fine weather. So a cowherd was needed—and Sarah was IT.

"Learning to do cheerfully the necessary jobs we really don't like to do is an important lesson in the school of life," Father told her last night.

School of life. Sarah lay on the meadow grass, her chin propped on her hand. She could hear the turf-turf-turf sound of cattle grazing. A breeze whistled in her ears, so the hum of the threshing machine only a quarter of a mile away sounded miles off. But every once in a while the machine whistle blew. It had a code of signals that every thresher understood. Every time the whistle blew, Sarah's spine tingled.

School of life. Sarah thought of school. Something exciting had happened the other day, something that had changed a lot of things. Mr. Thatcher came into the yard to pick up little Stella. She was eight years old and in grade two—but she was the tiniest child in Braeburn. Her father had been in town, hauling wheat to the elevator, so he was driving the lumber wagon.

Stella was perched on a seat, high in the air, when Mr. Thatcher remembered he had to ask Bertie Gerrick a question. Usually he could trust his horses to stand without being told. But a lot of boys and girls came running and shouting— they were so glad school was over—and the horses began moving. Stella grabbed one rein—just one. That scared the horses. They began running in circles in the yard.

Mr. Thatcher shouted whoa! and the children screamed. Then someone ran straight into the path of the team—they were behaving like broncs now—and jumped up and grabbed hold of their bridles and hung on, talking firmly. It was Miss Wentworth! She brought them to a stop, then held her arms up for Stella who tumbled into them. They hugged each other.

That moment something curious happened. All the children had seen. All of them thought Stella was sort of special. And perhaps Miss Wentworth had saved her life. Mr. Thatcher thought so and said so. And all the boys and girls looked at Teacher with new respect. It was a funny thing, but ever since then, things had been better at Braeburn. When people like you, you like them—and the more liking there is around, the better things go. That was one lesson Sarah had learned.

She thought soberly about some of the other lessons she had learned this summer. The events were exciting—or funny—or sad—all mixed up. But you could learn from every one. She remembered the day Spencer died—and the coming of Bouncer. He was almost running his legs off today. *He* liked to be where the excitement was too. And he agreed with Sarah that cows were very everydayish. But he didn't feel right about leaving Sarah alone on the job. So he trotted back and forth, back and forth— Right now his cold, moist nose touched her face briefly. Then he trotted off again, his tail waving behind him happily.

Sarah remembered the coming of the Chernishenkos—and the mystery of the hidden boy! And she remembered the hail-storm in the spring, when she and Robbie thought there'd be no crops this year. *Now* look at the fields! And she thought of the summer holidays—especially of the day when she and Susan and Linda had gone berry picking with Mrs. Slocum. Now Mrs. Slocum was dying. Everybody said she couldn't last much longer.

But she would! For ever and ever and ever!

Sarah rolled over on her back. She looked up, miles up, into the blue.